Just a Birdhouse

Just a Birdhouse

Emily Fohr

Desert Palm Press

Just a Birdhouse

By Emily Fohr

©2022 Emily Fohr

ISBN (trade) 9781948327596
ISBN (epub) 9781948327602

Desert Palm Press
1961 Main Street, Suite 220
Watsonville, California 95076
www.desertpalmpress.com

Editor: CK King
Cover Design: Michelle Brodeur

Printed in the United States of America
First Edition April 2022

Acknowledgements

I'd like to thank my dad for his steady guidance, countless revisions, and endless support. I'd like to thank my mom for the hours of French and English translated, spoken, and even argued. It was much needed. Lastly, I'd like to thank my family overseas, helping me with the unknown. Merci beaucoup.

I adore you all.

Dedication

To my time spent driving down the coast with Laura.

Prologue

CORDUROY PAINTINGS OF SATIN bed sheets, and steel planted frames suspend apathetically, overpowered by the elegance of crown moldings and the distant loathing confined inside the cherry-colored glass.

We came here to heal, but you left on the third day. The marble floors were too cold on your back, and you were afraid the crystallized chandelier would fall on our faces as we slept with the wind. You left.

I stayed because I knew the chandelier would come crashing down. I wanted to watch as the gelled diamonds rolled across the floor, dancing with rebellion, sparkling with unease.

Four iced chairs, stitched together by fire blown glass, sit abruptly in the middle of the parlor. Unable to mend their empty seats, they converse coolly with one another, hiding their scratches and refusing to admit why the ground below them is turning blue.

Magnificent windows, etched in the paneling, bear witness to the uncanny assembly set amidst the wide and intemperate dining hall. Empty of all its contents, the quad of chairs ignores one another now, concerned with who might be looking in.

On the terrace, a table set for seven. I'm not afraid of ghosts anymore. When they soar above and around me, I sway with them. Yearning for gratitude, they are the ones I beg to stay.

Half-filled wine glasses waver in tandem. Drunk with the spirits, I make a toast, never speaking aloud. They hear my thoughts and dance in agreement.

Barren bedrooms, arranged with care, wait for fallen footsteps to break their beautiful preservation. Sauntering around the upstairs suite, where intervals of existence have chosen to stay, I breathe in deeply. Our summer dream.

Japanese keys filled with bubbles and pauses of cherry blossoms tumble across the balcony, outstretched before the gentle armoire, decorated lavishly with your grandmother's antique porcelain china.

I refuse to breathe when I'm in this room. Somehow, I feel as though I'll defile what's been kept clean and persistent for so long.

Transcendent memories remind me that the south of France is a collection of unspoken sentiment, passion rooted in the reveries of late-night promenades and melting custard.

Chapter One

IN KEEPING WITH TRADITION, Appoline came to me in the night. She had heard from her mother who had spoken to Monsieur Fortin, the owner of the boulangerie, that my family was visiting Saint __ de Vie once again. Monsieur Fortin always baked in threes. Since my grandfather had surprised me with a brilliantly large gâteau Basque earlier that morning, only two were left under the warm glow of the bakery lights.

Amélie, Appoline's mom, was a curt and faintly woman, always afraid of running out of things she hadn't any need for. Upon seeing that one of the gâteaux Basque had been sold, she immediately had Monsieur Fortin wrap up the other two, one vanilla flavored and one dazzled with lemon zest.

Full and content, with a belly of my favorite black cherry gâteau Basque, I was lying in bed when Appoline rounded up the pathway to my grandfather's cottage. Patiently weathered on the seaside, his lodge was a wide open, summery affair. Even in winter, when the waves crashed below and sent chilly fog to kiss the windows, the house emanated warmth and comfort.

The summer was breezy in 1990, and the seaside village capitalized on fishing and tourism; catching Americans in the harbor, bringing them to shore tangled in giant nets, and ushering them to the coastal resort uphill. Hôtel Alarie was where the village's most pertinent guests came to stay and experience the 'posh' side of a town proud of their reputation for harvesting *beaucoup de poissons*. Fish were a passion here, not a pastime.

When I was younger, I had always begged my mom to stay a night at the Hôtel Alarie. She'd brush my hair and laugh, her breath of lavender cream.

"Bellamy," she'd whisper. "Papaly's house here is so much closer to the sea. If we stayed at the hotel, we'd have to walk five miles to get to the shore every single morning. Here, we can wake up and sit with our toes in the sand as we watch the sun rise."

Chin in my speckled hands, I painted sandcastles in my mind. "Sometimes I like to take walks though, maman."

I remember her nodding and digesting this information, as though it were a very wise thought. Twisting my bangs out of my face, she sighed.

"Well, the hotel is filled with people. We have this house all to ourselves."

Shrugging, I turned to face her. "Sometimes I like people."

The very next week, we were waltzing into the Hôtel Alarie, with a room booked and no reservations about us. It wasn't until a few days later, when my grandmother was scolding my mom for spoiling me, that I met Appoline Alarie, twelve-year-old heiress to the hotel that financed my dreams.

With a fistful of crumbling gâteau Basque, I had sprinted away from the coastal cabin and made my way down to the harbor. Mamaly, my grandmother, was speaking very quickly and loudly in French, admonishing my mom for letting me eat too much. I'd turn out greedy, she'd said.

Humming a tune that I had heard in the hotel lobby, I found myself sitting at the end of the dock, savoring my buttery pastry. The cusp of nightfall teased the horizon. Behind me, I heard footsteps. Appoline stood there, eyeing me curiously.

"*Tu n'as pas froid?*" *Aren't you cold?* she had asked forcefully.

I turned and shrugged.

"Oh, do you not speak French?"

Squinting at this bold girl, I grew stubborn.

"*Bonjour, je m'appelle* Bellamy," I said, defiant.

Standing to shake her hand, I smiled. The ice cream cone she was holding had begun to drip down her arm.

"Your French isn't bad, but I think my English is better. You have crumbs on your mouth by the way," she said, preoccupied with carelessly taking in the view of boats shimmering on the water.

"What's your name? There's ice cream on your elbow by the way." I stared her straight in the eyes with this response.

There was something so calm and steady about her demeanor, I wasn't even angry at her absence of tactful conversation. She told me her name was Appoline. We swapped sticky treats and sat on the edge of the dock, feet dangling.

"How do you know how to speak English so well?" I asked, smacking my lips.

"My mother is American. She moved here to marry my dad. Why is your French so bad?"

I took great offense to this but learned quickly that Appoline never meant any harm. She was just unaware of how blatantly direct she was. I told her my parents were divorced and that I came to France every summer with my mom.

"You know, it's my birthday today," I whispered, blushing.

I sat on top of my hands because I couldn't stop moving them. Appoline jumped up at this and grabbed me by the armpits. She dragged me into town and bought me an ice cream to celebrate.

"Any flavor! Pick one!" she screamed with delight.

"Okay, chocolate." I was embarrassed, yet excited that someone else was so excited about my birthday.

"No, no, no! You have to pick a flavor you've never had before, otherwise, where's the fun?" Appoline was insistent.

After indulgently slurping down apricot custard, I offered her the last bite.

"About time!" she said and grabbed the cone.

I celebrated my tenth birthday, skipping down the cobblestone roads of Saint __ de Vie, holding hands with Appoline. With flushed cheeks and rosy merriment, I pointed out my grandparents' cottage to her. She adored it.

"Looks peaceful. Away from everyone." Her eyes glistened with jealousy. Appoline kissed me once on each cheek, and I pinched her chin good night.

I returned home that evening to a room of villagers, large eyes, and swollen hands. My grandmother had died while I was out enjoying the return of the moon, the brisk evening air settling in my braids. The funeral was an abrupt conclusion to that summer, leaving us regretting how careless we had been. Black dresses and cold stones signified a dark end to what had always been so bright and vivid.

My mother and I continued our summer visits to Saint __ de Vie, until I was fourteen. We tried to console my grandfather, who refused to accept the very deep and very profound weight of loss he wore on his shoulders. It pushed him down, slumped him over, and made him a hunchback.

We stopped celebrating my birthday after my grandmother died. My mom would sneak me presents in the early morning, and my grandfather always left me a card with money under my door, but we never spoke about the inevitable aging that accrued with each passing year. My mother and grandfather would spend the day mourning.

I'd sit with them until my guilt snuck up my throat and choked me. Then when the silky breath of twilight set in, I'd slip out the bedroom bay window to meet Appoline, who was always cheery and always ready to buy me an ice cream cone of new and mysterious flavors.

Chapter Two

FIRST, THERE WAS A knock. I was floating somewhere, caught uneasily between the jagged pester of jetlag and the serenity of bristling lilacs on my night table which begged me to succumb to a deeper and deeper stupor. There was another knock as I wrestled the comforter and turned on the lamp which sat restfully next to the lilacs.

The bay window was directly behind the pillows on my bed. The French doors, which opened outward, were almost always ajar. I liked the smell of the sea to slide between my dreams at night and infect my thoughts. Rolling over onto my stomach, I pushed open the windows, aggressive rainfall soaking my sheets.

Sitting cross-legged in the open field that ran down to the sea, blissfully unaware that violent rain was pouring down, Appoline stretched out her arms beside her, holding hands with the grass. For a brilliant second, I didn't recognize her. Twenty-four. For some strange reason, her maturity took me by surprise.

She was wearing light-washed denim jeans, the kind that didn't look expensive but definitely were, a flowy Hawaiian button-down, and sandals. Dark brown hair hung dramatically around her, skimming her elbows playfully. Her collared shirt was open just enough to be provocative, but not enough to turn heads in an immodest way. Heads always turned to peer at Appoline, but only because her smile forced life on you and her laugh spun a thousand times over in your mind.

It was strange watching her from my window. When we were children, she always looked older than she was, chin held high, and inhibitions exhausted. Now, she held her age as a socialite who had grown into her cheekbones and sense of class. A thin, gold chain tapered her neck, no emblem hanging from it.

With her hair plastered to her face, she looked over at me as I hunched inside the warmth and safety of my comforter.

"Bonjour, ma chérie!" Hello, my darling! she called to me through the rain. She sat so calmly amongst the terror of mother nature that I was obliged to laugh.

7

"Well, are you going to come out and kiss me hello?" Appoline shouted.

"Appoline! It's raining!" I yelled from my cotton cocoon.

"So? You'll dry!" Appoline winked at me and laid back in the grass, arms still outstretched beside her.

Wearing my comforter as a shawl, I slipped out the bay window and ran across the grass, skidding with integrity and glee all the way there, all the way to Appoline. I sprawled out next to her, my back on the ground as I looked up into the rain, trying to see what she saw. A moment passed, and I politely decided to share my blanket with her. Tugging her from oblivion, she rolled over onto her stomach. Her face appeared above mine. I smiled.

"Bonjour, Appoline," I beamed. "C'est une nuit magnifique. Comment vas-tu?" It's a magnificent night, how are you? I asked.

I had been waiting to show off. Appoline squealed with joy and kissed my forehead.

"Bonjour, ma chérie. You've been practicing your French!"

Leaning back down, she kissed me on both cheeks. She was warm.

"I had to take four years of it to graduate high school. And another four to graduate college. But I am, as they say, a natural." Giggling, I spoke in my thickened French accent.

Appoline shook her head, lying back down next to me, under my beautifully drenched blanket.

"Bah, I forget! You've just finished at university. Such a baby!" Her arms were folded beneath her head.

Stars were barely visible that night, but by squinting, one could've easily confused raindrops for the infinite galaxy. Brazenly, I turned on my side to face her. She tried to hide a smile, knowing she'd provoked me.

"By all accounts, ma chérie, I am a woman! In your country and in mine." I proclaimed loudly to Appoline, to the rain, to the night.

She turned on her side to challenge me. "Let's go for a drink," she said.

My eyes must have widened, because as I was about to protest, she shook her head.

"Now?" I asked.

"Yes, now," she took my chin in her hands. "And stop with that horrible accent. You have insulted me in my country."

I laughed as she attempted to stand up, slipping on the slick lawn. Pulling her back down, I paused, realizing I was acting much too familiar with a girl I hadn't seen in eight years.

"How did you know I was back?" I questioned.

Appoline stared straight in my eyes, just as she always did, or maybe as I always did, fearlessly through the rain.

"Apparently *someone* bought a gâteau Basque from Monsieur Fortin this morning. No one ever buys a gâteau Basque." She rolled her eyes as she said this.

With that sentiment, Appoline was up and running toward town. I watched her in disbelief before understanding she wasn't any different at all. The vivacity of her youth was still there. I hung the darkened remains of my comforter on the windowsill and ran after her, hoping I wasn't any different, either.

"Well, at least I know your mom hasn't changed! My gâteau Basque was delicious by the way, thanks for asking," I called after her, through the endless torrent of pouring rain.

Chapter Three

WE RACED ALL THE way to the pub in town, jumping over cracks in the weaving road. A creeping sensation that Appoline was trying to avoid talking to me jabbed at my gut, but I was soaking wet in my pullover, so I decided to let this thought slip over me.

Inside the pub, the air was dry, and the light was different. I could see the brown skin on Appoline's cheeks. What had once been so rosy was now smooth and mature, like perfumed myrrh. We sat in a booth. No one turned to look at us. Everyone was wet.

That night, I took ten shots of Cointreau, partly because I was nervous, but mostly because Appoline kept encouraging me to and I didn't want to insult her.

After our first two shots, we had barely spoken. So much time had passed since we'd seen each other; I wasn't sure if we'd even still get along. The first two shots went down easily and quite quickly for both of us. Appoline was anxious, constantly scanning the room as if waiting for someone unwelcome to appear. After she ordered two more shots, a group of men walked into the pub. Their leather jackets profusely sweat rain all around us. Popping her head out, she caught the eye of a particularly tall and broad member of the group.

His name was Jean-Marc, and from what I could make out by eavesdropping, his parents knew Appoline's parents. I realized, the second he raised his finger to address the bartender and ask for the most expensive Scotch they had, that he was the type of guy who spent his summers gambling away his trust fund in Monte Carlo.

Once Appoline remembered to introduce me, I politely greeted him with kisses on both cheeks. He asked if we wanted to join him and his friends for drinks. They were all celebrating Jean-Marc and his father's buyout of a finance firm uptown. Why were they partying in our small village of Saint __ de Vie, I wondered? I was sure there were many clubs inland that would serve their intentions much better. Well, Appoline explained to me, it was the only place they could get rowdy without risking the chance of being recognized.

My chest clenched. I was soaking wet, sleep deprived, and in no way prepared to have drunken conversations in French with a group of financiers I had just met. Thankfully, Appoline declined the offer, saying she was catching up with an old friend.

I'm not sure why, but this phrasing angered me deep down, in a way it definitely shouldn't have, so I took my third shot without her, while she said goodbye to Jean-Marc. There was something very sensuous about her manner and ease. Her ability to look clean while brutally wet, and forgiving while in men's clothing, flustered everyone who peered over Jean-Marc's shoulder, interested now in the dame who had taken over the small pub, glowing with congeniality.

"Oh." She sat back down and looked at the empty shot glass. "Drink the other one, too. I ordered them both for you." She smiled softly at me.

"You're not drinking anymore?" My voice cracked as I coughed to cover my confusion.

"Oh, *ma chérie*, I'd already had half a bottle of wine before I came to your house. Why do you think I was so warm in the pouring rain?"

I grabbed the fourth shot lightly in between my thumb and forefinger, beginning to feel gratitude toward my friend of many summers. I raised the glass.

"To the heiress." I downed the Cointreau and leaned forward, whispering. "I didn't realize you were an alcoholic now."

Appoline bent her chest across the table, matching me and whispering back, her flowy shirt falling slightly open.

"The French are never alcoholics. We are just...enthusiasts." She smiled and picked up my empty shot glass, pressing it to her lips. Raising an eyebrow, she licked the edge and then tipped it into her mouth.

"You didn't get all of it." Still whispering, she set the clean glass in front of me.

For a moment, I sat there, then realized if ever there were a time for banter, it was now.

"Well, I guess I'll need two more then," I smiled slyly.

Appoline banged her fists on the table in agreement. "*Oui, bien sûr!*"

Her hair was drying in a chaotic mess of strays. "*Excusez-moi! Deux de plus, s'il vous plaît!*"

Once I had licked my fifth and sixth shots clean to Appoline's approval, the pub was beginning to feel more conversant. Any sense of caution I had imagined I needed was blown away, fried, and disintegrating in the steamy yellow lights hanging above us.

Appoline sat cross-legged on her side of the booth. I leaned against the wall, my legs up on the wooden bench. After chugging a glass of room-temperature water, I sighed, biting my tongue.

"Oh, no, no. No complaining about the water. You Americans are so spoiled with your cold water," she grunted, wagging her finger at me.

"Appoline." I was warm now and trying to speak levelly. "It just tastes so much better cold. It's refreshing."

"The body can get used to anything, Bellamy. By the time you leave here, you'll be ordering waters with no ice, once again."

I chuckled. "It's not even that. When the water is ice cold, I can drink two glasses, straight away. Now, I drink one and don't even want to bother with another."

Smiling proudly and knowingly, Appoline nodded her head. "See, this water quenched your thirst. It's better." She looked over to me, somehow more at ease. "So, Bellamy, eight years, and you forget to visit? What happened? Where have you been? Who has been buying you ice cream on your birthday while you've been away?"

At this, I swung my feet onto the ground and turned, once again, to face her. I couldn't stop smiling, and I could feel the heat from my cheeks rising.

"So, Appoline, eight years. I didn't forget to visit. I don't know...things just got...busy."

She raised her eyebrows and waved her hand for me to continue.

"I don't know. The summer I turned fifteen, I stayed home to get my driver's permit and got my first job as a hostess at a movie theater. The summer I turned sixteen, I stayed home because I wanted to get my license, since all my friends already had theirs. The summer I turned seventeen, my dad's side of the family had a reunion. The last four years, I've been in college. I'm telling you, nothing special, things just got..." My voice trailed off.

"Busy," she said, finishing my sentence.

I couldn't look into her eyes. Somehow, I knew she was hurt.

"But I'll have you know, no one bought me ice cream a single year I was gone," I added.

This seemed to perk her up.

"Well, I guess we have eight years' worth of ice cream eating to make up for." She kicked her foot underneath the table, brushing my knee.

"Anyway," I coughed. "Enough about my boring American

summers. What about you? Twenty-four! Did you go to university? What are you doing now? Tell me everything."

There was a halt in her glowing demeanor. She shrugged and called the barman for two more shots. I laughed uneasily.

"Appoline, are you trying to get me drunk?"

"You need to catch up to me, and talking won't get you there," she smirked.

I saluted her as I took shots number seven and eight. The orange liqueur sailed smoothly down my throat, burning only my nose. The acidity of the citron scent smacked me in the face with memories of childhood adventures, scraped knees, fluorescent scarves, flower picking contests. I looked over, smiling iridescently. Appoline had her head tilted sideways.

"What?" I asked.

"You're remembering." She pulled back the lapel on her shirt, revealing the pointed collarbones I had always been so jealous of. Cracked into place, they looked like jewels, cradling her neck. Above her left collarbone sat a rigid scar, white and loud against her brown complexion. Pointing at it, I took a sip of water that was no longer there.

"That, now that was the day Eloise and, who was it? Gerard? Yeah, that was the day we were all playing tag and you swam into the sea. I remember."

Appoline giggled, her eyes lighting up with superfluous musings of the past. "Gerard threw a rock at me—"

"That bastard was just too scared to swim after you."

We both paused, shocked at how cleanly my opinion filtered through my mouth. Laughing, Appoline shook her head, shadowy hair hiding the scar.

"You were always so jealous of him."

"No, I wasn't! I—he—Appoline! He threw a rock at you in the water, saying that if it touched you, you were 'it.' He didn't want to get his fancy little plaid shorts wet. I remember. And you needed five stitches because of it!" I crossed my arms and sat back against the wooden booth.

"See, jealous," she said lightly.

"You—you held hands with him all the way to the hospital." After seeing the look in her eyes, I laughed, realizing how bitter I sounded. "Okay, okay, I get it," I surrendered.

Rolling her fingers back and forth on the table, she suddenly thrust herself up and ran out the door, leaving me, for what I thought was forever.

Moments later, she strolled back into the pub, shoulders rounded and pupils keen. I sat on the edge of my seat, playing along with her game.

"I like this song. I wanted to walk out and walk back in, as if I were hearing it for the first time. Come on, dance with me," she gleamed.

I looked around. It was about two-thirty in the morning, and people had begun to shuffle out. The villagers that remained consisted of a few fishermen, a girl who I remembered from my youth but whose name I couldn't exactly pin, and three townies, playing pool by the jukebox. The horde of posh men that Appoline knew had taken over a corner and were enjoying a game of ruthless beer chugging.

Gathering myself, I stood and walked out the door, copying Appoline and leaving her in the center of the bar, alone. As soon as I stepped outside, I let the unused mist that lingered in the air fall on my face. Now, my sweat looked like angel's breath.

Waltzing back inside, I strutted boldly up to Appoline, who was standing exactly where I'd left her.

"Wow, you know what?" I asked snootily.

"What?" Her eyes bounced up and down; she was enthralled with it all.

I took a step closer to her. "I absolutely adore this song, too. Let's dance?"

Appoline laughed with pure excitement, and I realized everything I did was to hear her laugh, even if it was just for a second.

"It would be a shame not to! *Bon alors*, dance!" she declared.

Clapping her hands, she spun in a circle, dancing unevenly to the music. Precariously, I danced next to her, the liqueur giving me a sense of courage I had never been able to find on my own. We laughed and spun and sang until our words mixed together and I didn't know who was saying what, and it truly didn't matter.

"What's this song called?" I asked her, wanting to remember the way it stole my inhibitions.

"No clue! This is the first time I've heard it." Appoline mused. Her hands above her head, she shrugged at me. "I just thought it sounded pretty!"

The men in the corner noticed the tenacity in our carelessness, and they appreciated it. Growing rather sweaty, I took off my pullover and threw it on a table nearby. The spaghetti straps of my tank top were drenched with perspiration. Appoline let out a gaudy laugh.

"Bellamy," she shrieked, pinching my hips. "You aren't a chubby little girl anymore. Look at you!"

I did a twirl for her benefit.

"Oh, look, I'm not the only one who's noticed your shape." She pointed behind me, winking, as I turned around to see Jean-Marc and two of his friends walking haughtily toward us.

Whispering loudly in a beautiful waterfall of cascading French, the young financiers, ripe with ambition, sang to us sweetly with their endearing words. Playing along, we danced blithely through the night, swinging from arm to arm. During one particularly rowdy song, the barman stood atop the counter, conducting his way through drinks and cheers.

Jean-Marc, red and giddy, whispered to Appoline, brushing her hair behind her ear. I looked away, embarrassed. Appoline, uninterested, didn't bother to stop dancing. She shrugged and grabbed my elbow.

"Jean-Marc wants to buy us shots!" she told me over the blaring radio.

"Oh, no. I've already had…" Before I was able to finish, Jean-Marc shoved a shot into my hand, smiling proudly.

"*Pour vous!*" He motioned for me to drink it, and I hastily shot the Cointreau back.

"*Merci!*" I yelled, holding back the burn smearing the edges of my eyes.

He grinned and kissed both my cheeks before dancing away. Coughing, Appoline appeared, handing me another shot.

"*Tiens.* Here, take this. It's for you." She was sweaty and out of breath, exulting in the vibrant evening.

I told her I had already drunk mine. I was nine shots deep. She wouldn't accept this answer.

"You must make it ten! An even number, I insist."

Her eager eyes watched me down the shot. She was overjoyed. I was beaming.

The dancing lasted until about four in the morning. Around three, when the spirits were charging my body with vigor, I realized just how close we all really were. Claude and Martin swayed on either side of me, the girl from my childhood whose name I couldn't remember, stood numbly in front of the bar, tapping her foot. Appoline, eyes closed, tenderly caressed Jean-Marc's arms as she fell back into him. He held her hips in place until the song changed and her head was flowing, bobbing around us all, a commune of drunken souls. Lumbering over to the bar, I ordered an eleventh shot of Cointreau. Just as the music began to sound too melodic and the air became too easy to breathe, the introspection of life painted around me turned hazy.

Someone pinched my hips and grabbed the glorious glass of drink from my hand. Cheekily, Appoline wrapped her arm around my shoulders and summoned me outside.

The misty night had decided to pale under the dotting of streetlamps, and I shivered in rhythm to the remnants of the song that lingered past the storefront. Appoline, leaning against the brick exterior, sighed and drank the shot I'd ordered. Her slim figure, aching and sullen under the speckling of fog and cigarette smoke, beckoned romance and desire.

"That was my shot, you know," I pirouetted on tiptoe, lightly allowing the evening's discourse of tumbling words, brazen men, and held breath to stain my smile.

Amused, Appoline shook her head, sighing again.

"Well, this time it was my turn to catch up to you." She winked slyly. She was always winking.

Appalled, I teased her. The famous heiress, Appoline, a drunkard! Was it possible she was *still* sober? I grabbed her hand and twirled her around, our cheeks reddened, and the air filled with echoes of our jolly humming. We danced gaily outside the front window, coated with warm condensation and wandering eyes. Laughing, she leaned back against the wall.

"I'm so glad you're back, Bellamy. It's good to see you." Opening a pack of cigarettes, she offered me one.

"Oh, I don't smoke," I said, trying to catch my breath.

"Me either," she mumbled, and lit her cigarette, sucking in profoundly, exhaling life.

"You are such a cliché," I giggled.

For a brief moment of silence, I feared I had offended her with my candor. Instead, she let out a roaring guffaw, lit two more cigarettes and held all three to her lips.

"*Excusez-moi! Pardon, ma chérie*, but I am no clue what you mean by zis. Oh, one moment, I seem to 'ave forgotten *mon béret* at my apartment in Paris!" Her French accent was strong and ridiculous, mocking me. I burst into laughter. She nodded.

"French maybe, but don't you dare ever call me a cliché, Bellamy Artois! You are the cliché, running away to a summer home on the Côte de Lumière each summer." She rolled her eyes.

Somnolent, I chuckled in agreement. She had a point. She always did. "What gave me away? My American accent?" I played along.

"*Non*, you got drunk off four shots, only Americans get drunk that quickly." The smoke from her cigarette frosted the air.

"Appoline, I've taken ten shots!"

"*Oui*, but you've been drunk since number four!" Appoline squealed and we both doubled over with laughter.

"Here, you look cold. Take this sweater." She handed me a woolen sweater that I hadn't noticed her wearing before. "It's Jean-Marc's, but he won't mind you wearing it."

Quietly, I said merci.

"Are you...?" I cut back on my question.

"We are friends. Jean-Marc is a good friend. You'll like him. He's much less uptight than Gerard, don't worry."

"Bastard," I whispered sarcastically under my breath.

She appreciated my humor. Appoline took a drag from all three cigarettes, discarded them under her brown sandal that was torn at the edges, and somehow, we ended up back inside.

After saying farewell and kissing every villager four times on each cheek before remembering we had already said farewell and kissed each cheek of each villager an appropriate number of times, Appoline and I meandered back up toward the cottages.

Town was about a three-mile stretch from the small seaside homes that sat on the cliffs of rushing waves. The harbor lay in between, full of dipping boats and sandy expanses, making the beach a gloomy, yet passionate affair. About another three miles past the beach and above the cottages were the hotels and resorts rooted in greed and tourism.

A muddle of mist clothed the spread before us, making the tiny footpaths feel even tinier. Arriving at my grandfather's lodge, I could spot the sun peeking over the horizon. My billowy comforter was hanging from the bay window, damp and dirty. Morning dew and spots of small sunrays lit the apples of Appoline's cheeks. She grinned at me as I yawned, nudging her head toward the hill where her hotel waited patiently and quietly for her.

"I'd better get back before maman wakes up and sees I'm gone. She'll probably have breakfast set and ready by the time I walk in the door," she said.

"A gâteau Basque I'm hoping?" My banter was dwindling, as I fought to keep my eyes from closing.

"If my jeans get tighter this summer, I know who to blame,

Bellamy." She laughed and kissed me on both cheeks with the same tenacity she had five hours earlier.

"Go, go. Your château awaits," I teased.

As she twirled and floated away, she left me with the rich scent of chamomile and linen. The simplicity of clean adoration smelled so good.

"Oh, shit. Appoline!" I began to run after her, flourishing grass all around me. I almost slipped as I wrenched Jean-Marc's sweater off my back. Turning around to face me, but never stopping in stride, she waved.

"Keep it!" she shouted.

Without waiting for my response, she whirled around gracefully, Hawaiian shirt flowing behind her, jeans stained wet just underneath the back pockets, cupping her bottom.

Crawling through the bay window, into the whitewashed walls and paneled floors of my bedroom bungalow, I stripped to my underwear. Piled in the corner of the room were my wet clothes and dirty blanket.

The birds were beginning to wake, and the sea was once again stirring. Asleep, under cotton sheets, I caressed the woolen sweater, my fingers caught in the frays. It was his, but it smelled like her.

Chapter Four

SURROUNDED BY AN INCESSANT tranquility and the infinite calm that lives on the sea, my dreams that first night were disturbed only by the swooping of distant seagulls and the smell of bold espresso brewing in the kitchen adjacent to me.

I stumbled sleepily to the pantry, cozy in my thoughts and content with the tenderness only a deep slumber can provide. After pouring a liberal amount of espresso into a tiny mug that hung from a rack above the counter, I snuggled beside my mom, who was knitting in her spot by the sun.

She was an elegant fixture in the kitchen nook. My grandfather sat peacefully across from her in a timber-backed rocking chair, reading the newspaper. Unaware I was yawning, I saw him shake his head in disapproval. Sneaking me a smile, my mom stretched and offered me the quilt from her lap.

Nine in the morning was timid on *la côte*. Drowsy villagers took meaningless walks as they waited for the sun to glow with its summer ferocity. I watched from the window as tourists with kites ran down the beach and vendors with fancier kites sprinted after them. My mother, grandfather, and I sat together, content and relaxed. We were a quiet three, pleased with our company, understanding there wasn't always a need for persistent conversation. Just *being,* was enough.

After my second overflowing cup of espresso, my grandfather brought over three éclairs, one for each of us.

"Monsieur Fortin must've been expecting us," my mother said.

My mom cherished her chocolate éclair, as I shoved mine greedily down my throat. I had never been one to savor anything. Papaly chuckled at my engorged cheeks, happy to see me happy.

"I thought we could walk into town today, buy some postcards at the market, grab lunch?" my mom continued.

She held up her square of yarn for us to see. My grandfather grunted in response.

"What is that?" I asked, intrigued by the awfully woven varying of blues.

My mom squinted her eyes, staring at the unfortunate mess before her. "I'm not sure...we'll see, I guess."

She smiled and set it down. Papaly, speaking for the first time, muttered something under his breath that sounded like, "You try every year, it's okay to be bad at something."

Papaly didn't speak any English, and my French was poor. We relied on my mom to translate for us, but mostly, we sat quietly together, always enjoying the company.

I traipsed back to my private suite in the rear of the house, jittery from caffeine and the expectations of a tanned-skin, chocolate éclair-eating summer. Quickly, I brushed my teeth and washed my face. The guest bathroom was kept bleached and unused. Though it had been years, Papaly couldn't bring himself to clean out my grandmother's things.

After thoroughly scrubbing my face, I doubled over, feeling the citrus mistakes of the night before creeping up my throat. Once I was absolutely certain I was done profusely throwing up, I propped my knees up to my chin, leaning against the tiled bathtub.

I had gotten drunk in France for the first time. I knew I was smiling. I felt so much older than I was before. Quiet moments of accomplishment came in pauses as I searched for something to wear, as I applied rouge to my cheeks, as I handwashed my comforter, coaxing the rebellion from it.

For some reason, college frat parties did not have the same sense of romance that the village pub did. I should have gone out more when I was in school, but I was always too caught up in grades and who was giving them to me. A brief stint of my schooling was controlled by the eager crushes I had on my English professors. Every single one. I had always allowed my imagination to roam freely, which left my real life sitting complacently on the back burner. I'd rather dream it than experience it, that was the conclusion I had come to.

Jumping down the steps of the cottage, I raced over to my mom and Papaly, who were waiting patiently, their toes straddling the cobblestone pathway and the sand on the other side. I had brushed my hair up into a bun, the short, layered pieces outlining my face.

It was a hot day, but I wore Jean-Marc's sweater. The sleeves were rolled, and my denim shorts were loose enough to allow me to eat without guilt. I walked hand in hand with my mom. We pointed at canoes and took pictures of the waves. Papaly bought me a coconut pastry as he walked his girls proudly into town.

Monsieur Fortin was much younger than I remembered. To a thirteen-year-old girl, anyone called monsieur must've been as old as my grandfather. The trick of words on the psyche is quite a peculiar thing. Monsieur Fortin looked to be in his late thirties, a rough layer of hair coating a jawline that I knew was strong. Each woman who walked into his boulangerie stared unashamed with lustful eyes, buying much more than they needed.

Monsieur Fortin's poise and eloquence, a kind that only a baker of tiny pastries and fluffy crèmes could attain, either masked his arrogance or proved he didn't have any at all. It was hard for me to believe that a man could be ogled at as persistently as he and remain so supremely oblivious as to why his macarons sold out on the daily. The three of us walked into his shop, Papaly directing us with a sense of urgency I had never seen from him before.

Once the bell above the door rang and Monsieur Fortin rushed to greet us, my grandfather's intentions became very clear. In rapid French, I caught pieces of stifled conversation. My quiet Papaly grunted here and there, allowing Monsieur Fortin to make questioning statements. One grunt meant yes; two grunts meant no. My mom blushed when he kissed her twice. Embarrassed for her, I looked at the swelling loaves of bread before remembering my manners.

Courteously, I let Monsieur Fortin kiss my cheeks, standing on tiptoe so he didn't have any reason to bend down. My mom gave me an obvious nudge with her hip. She talked superfluously to him, my name in every other sentence. The instigator of this excessively chatty mess stood behind us, arms crossed, delighted. I rolled my eyes at him, but Papaly avoided my glare. The pleased matchmaker smiled down at his shoes. He hadn't brought us here for baked goods, he'd brought us here to meet Monsieur Fortin. I could only imagine what my grandfather had told him about me.

When it was time to order, my grandfather insisted I practice my French and do it myself. Had it not been for my profound shock, I would've put up more of a fight. Unfortunately, I was left to fend for myself. My mother hid suspiciously behind the row of tartes, and my grandpa walked out of the shop, waving goodbye to Monsieur Fortin, before I had even asked for the baguette that apparently, *he* wanted so badly.

"*Une baguette, s'il vous plaît.*" I said to Monsieur Fortin, who had now resumed his place behind the counter.

"*C'est tout?*" *Is that all?* he asked. He looked imploringly into my eyes, as if the fate of his livelihood rested in my hands.

Annoyed and thoroughly disappointed in myself, I strode out of the store with a baguette in my hand and three macarons I didn't even want. I thrust the baguette at my grandpa, who laughed heartily. Dismayed, my mom scolded me.

"What? Papaly wasn't actually hungry for another baguette! He just wanted to show us off to Monsieur Fancypants!"

My neck twitched as I covered my face. To this, Papaly wagged his finger and told me he is always hungry for another baguette. My mom broke off a piece of fresh crust and stuffed it into her mouth, insisting that I'd forgotten to mention Monsieur Fortin had indeed given me the macarons for free.

Chapter Five

LUNCH WAS A MUCH more moderate affair. After devouring the baguette and all three macarons, I had decided to put my unreasonable dislike for Monsieur Fortin to bed and my shame to ease. My mom had promised not to bring him up anymore. The free pastries were quite delicious, melting on my tongue so delicately, I couldn't help but wonder why I had always hated macarons.

Our walk back home led us to shore, but first I stopped at La Baleine Bleue, the pub from the night before. In the daylight, the exterior was much less romantic. The stubborn siding was gnarled, and the nets that hung from the ceiling made the entire place feel like a nautical pun.

I asked the barman if he had found the sweater I had left there, but he told me a girl had stopped by earlier and picked it up. I thanked him with confusion and bounced back to my mother and grandfather, both of whom were tired now and sticky from the salty winds.

"I went out last night," I told my mother, as Papaly strolled serenely behind us, picking up pebbles and putting them in his pocket.

"Where? With whom?" Her brown hair rustled against her neck. When she asked things, she was always steady, never worried, never concerned.

"To the pub, in town here. Appoline heard from her mom that we were back, so she came and took me for a drink."

"Oh, Appoline. The little girl that was always running around. How is she?"

We stopped for a moment as I scooped her hair off her shoulders and swept it into a bun. I sat down next to her on the splintered bench, overlooking the dock where fishermen shouted across to one another, boat to boat. We watched Papaly search the sands like a toddler, hoping to find a gem amongst the rocks.

"Still running...she's fine. Anyway, I had left my sweater in the pub, so that's why I went back to ask if they had it."

I needed to work on not overexplaining. No one ever really cared why I did the things I did. My mom waved to Papaly as he began his ascent toward us.

"So, whose sweater is this?" she asked, pulling at the wool on my shoulder.

"Oh, Appoline's."

Outside the cottage, my grandpa bent over, setting a few of the stones he had collected on separate stairsteps. There was an assortment of rocks gathered there, outlining the path to the front door. My mother sighed and walked inside to shower. Slightly disheartened, Papaly looked at me, upturning his lips, then followed her in.

I spent what was left of the day unpacking my things and meticulously organizing. My desire for consolidation could be overpowering and, in all honesty, was probably due to some kind of tragic childhood trauma or lack of consistency therein. Combing through my belongings, I set Jean-Marc's woolen sweater on top of my suitcase, hidden in the back of the closet, where it was destined to spend the entirety of the summer.

Just before dinner time, Papaly knocked lightly on my door, humbly walking in. I was in the middle of spreading a new blanket on the bed. He eyed me suspiciously. Hanging from my bay window was the white comforter, drying in the tired breeze. I laughed as he put up his hand, waving off any explanation. With his other hand, he handed me a glass of wine. Striking his finger to his lips, he left just as quickly as he came. Mother was never to hear about this. I think rebellion is hereditary, though, so she must've always known.

Bloated from one too many glasses of red wine and the deepness of brie settling in my stomach, I arrived at dinner. My mom surprised us all with a bottle of champagne to toast our return. Reminiscing over photo albums, long talks, and the exuberance we found in one another, we ended the evening marching throughout the small living room with the *Les Misérables* soundtrack blaring.

Papaly fell asleep next to the French doors atop candied cushions, smiling in his dreams. Stretched out on the marmalade-blushed couch, my mom returned to her feeble attempt at knitting, and I kissed her goodnight before drifting off to my room. I was at ease here, sprawled out on my cotton bed, the sun setting behind me, kissing the waves *bonsoir*.

As I went to close my shutters, I saw my sweater I had left at the bar, hanging by a thread from the handle. Adoringly, I pulled it close to my heart, genuine happiness washing over my skin. I knew it wasn't the barman who had placed it there. I had only been on the Côte de Lumière one full day, and already I had been drunk twice, spoiled with pastries, and now I was one sweater richer.

Chapter Six

RISING EARLIER THAN I had the morning before, I set out just as the clouds decided to change color. Yearning for the magic of dewy 'in betweenness,' I took a walk down by the shore, slipping keenly to the place betwixt the water and the sky. My favorite time of day was when the coastline was bright, but the sun was still hidden.

In his younger years, my grandfather owned a wine shop. A connoisseur of sorts, he treasured the amiable depths of humanity, allowing the many kinds of people he met to teach him what it looked like to be a red wine drinker or a fan of bubbles and circumstance. Though he didn't speak much, he took in everything and everyone around him, nodding at their stories, grunting at the tales of travels and newborn babies and solemn burials.

With age grew his realization that many people shared their lives with him simply because he would listen. He sold the wine shop when he was thirty, married my grandmother and bought her a house on the coast, just as she had always wanted. Together, they raised my mom, planning to explore Eastern Europe once she left for college. This never came to be, though, as my grandmother developed a slight case of agoraphobia. Afraid to leave her cottage, she stuck to her home on the shore. It felt safe to her, so they never left.

Eventually, my grandfather opened shop once again, selling wine and spirits to the handsome and rugged people of Saint __ de Vie. Once my grandmother died, he sold the store. He retired out of regret, wishing he had spent more time with her, and less time surrounded by full bottles, just waiting to be consumed.

Despite his soft life, floating on the edge of deep breaths and repentance, Papaly still spent every Saturday hosting a wine tasting in the garden behind his old shop. Saul, the new owner, had begged him to do this. Affectionately, he looked up to Papaly, asking him to share his wealth of knowledge with the town, convinced his familiar face would keep generations of customers streaming in.

Papaly's genuine talent lay within others, though. He had this strange way of listening to you talk and being able to pinpoint exactly what kind of drink suited you best, even if you had never had it before.

My mother found this quite annoying, as he was constantly asking her to try new drinks every night. He blamed this on her frivolity and consistently inconsistent ways. In truth, my mother was kind and loving, she just always craved movement, probably a testament to the sedentary lifestyle she had growing up. Yet, she didn't resent her parents. In fact, the summers when we visited Saint __ de Vie, were the only times I ever saw her content with stillness, watching locals drift on the sea.

Entrenched in picturesque romances and improper getaways, my mother spent her time traveling the world, sailing to exotic places with exotic men. The summers were harmonious, holding the safe havens and rejuvenation of desire. We treasured these moments together, calmly in place, harboring sandy hair and pruned skin, which would take an entirety of the following year to get rid of.

Maybe it was my mother's perpetually unpredictable romantic life that made me stationary in my own. Perhaps I was merely waiting for my chance to follow in her footsteps. Whatever the case, I was sure to render our first trip back to Saint __ de Vie in eight years as an excuse to figure it all out. I knew this summer would be my opportunity to complete the unfinished moments from high school and college and each sporadic bout of passion I'd had in my past. I had been so close, many times before, but had never successfully done the deed, allowing insecurities or romanticization to sabotage the momentous event. I was determined not to stand in my own way any longer.

In poetic walks across the sand, I sauntered alone with the seagulls, happy because of it. Seldom was the time I needed others around me. Comfort was found in my independence, and though I had weak moments of wishful, passionate affairs, I craved the solitude these French summers gave me. I missed my friends across the waters but escaping to the cliffs and living discreetly amongst people who didn't recognize me always gave me a feeling of sweet solace. Seeing as I'd be returning to New York in the fall for my first job in professional America, I made sure to ignore all alarm clocks. I wanted to wake without being told to. I assumed it was well before six in the morning.

I made my way down to the dock, where boats bumped gently, slaves to the current. Amid the bows sweetly nipping at one another, I could see my grandmother's ghostly façade speaking quickly with my grandfather on a canoe. She was persistent in explaining that the buoy ten feet away would be as far as she could venture. He didn't push her, steering the blue boat back to the dock.

Clouds were floating without a care in the sky now, briny air brushing against my visage and massaging years of seaside chronicles into my skin. At the end of the pier, slumped over and wonderfully at peace with the crashing waters, was Appoline. Broken shards of glass sprinkled the perimeter around her ashen hair, splayed about the wooden slabs of cherry harbor. Quietly, I stepped around, holding my breath so as to not disturb her soft slumber.

Leaning back against the shafts of timber, I let my toes skim the water below. A seagull landed in front of me. I shooed her away just as Appoline stirred, gracefully awakening.

"Bellamy? How long have you been here?" Appoline didn't bother sitting up, she looked at me from her bed on the walkway.

"The real question, is how long have *you* been here?" I grinned, seamlessly hiding my hand in her hair.

"I've been here all night."

"Doing what?" I asked. I wanted to lie down next to her, but the broken glass was a fence, keeping me out.

"Reading, drinking, trying not to fall asleep." Her words were filled with warmth.

I noticed the wine bottle scattered haphazardly in fragments beside her novel. It was empty before the glass broke. No wine stained the wood.

"You look like you're waiting for someone," I suggested.

"I don't wait for anyone, Bellamy. If people decide to show up, it's a coincidence, not a plan gone right."

"You're always talking in riddles," I said.

"No, it's just my accent," she joked, stretching her arms above her head.

"Thanks for dropping off my sweater, by the way," I blushed.

"I would've stayed, but I figured only stalkers stay outside someone's window two nights in a row. I'm a drifter, not a romantic," Appoline replied.

Rolling my eyes, I picked up a piece of glass, smoothing it in the palm of my hand. "It's broken." I noted.

"You're always so painfully aware. Good thing I had already finished the bottle." Appoline laughed, standing up now and gathering the remaining shards and stuffing them in the quilted towel she had been using as a pillow.

"So," she said, hand on her hip. "What are we doing today?"

The certainty in her streaming consciousness caught me off guard. She was rather alert and bright eyed for someone who had spent the night sleeping half out of water, sipping wine. Appoline was already walking hastily down the dock. I grabbed the book she'd left sitting on the edge and ran after her.

"Oh, *merci*. I can't even begin to tell you how many books I've lost from forgetting them there."

After dumping the glass into a garbage can, she wrapped the towel around us, leading me back toward the beach.

"It's Saturday, so I was actually planning on going to my grandpa's wine tasting. Apparently, he hosts one every weekend at Aux vins de Malloren. In the garden."

Appoline kissed me on both cheeks so suddenly, I could feel my heart stutter.

"*Bon*, what time?" she inquired with eager eyes.

"Um, I think it starts at noon."

"Fantastic. I'll see you then. I must go shower now and see what maman has prepared for breakfast. Oh, and will you tell your grandpa to stop buying things in threes at Monsieur Fortin's? It's giving my mom a headache trying to keep up! Aye, is my tongue red?"

At this, she stuck out her tongue abruptly in front of my face, blocking my view of everything, other than her.

"Ahhhhhhhhh," she hummed, her tongue, colored brightly, reverberating against the back of her throat.

"Blood red." I swallowed.

"*Merde*." *Shit,* she cussed lightly, then squeezed my cheek and ran off, past the twirling streaks of sand and over the cliffs to Hôtel Alarie, the refuge that was always waiting for her, unmoving and distant.

The town's festive bustling grew with a light crescendo as the first of the villagers headed to market. I must've walked past Monsieur Fortin's boulangerie ten times before I gathered the courage to go in and order a bag of black currant macarons. The older woman who wrapped them pleasantly for me in orange tissue paper had kind, wrinkled eyes. She wiped her hands on her apron as I nodded my thanks and bounded by the row of scrumptiously bronzed madeleines.

Taking the scenic route to the door resulted in an inadvertent collision with Monsieur Fortin himself, who was exiting the kitchen, and who tirelessly insisted I call him François. Mortified, I realized I had managed to spit frothy chunks of his own macaron all over his front side. Choking out my apologies, I ran from the shop, embarrassed at how unfazed he seemed.

Decorated with the result of too many human interactions long before the sun had settled securely in her place in the sky, I ran back to the cottage and let my grandpa pour me a regulation sized espresso, heaving at my unfortunate luck. By the time Papaly and I were jumping on our bikes to head back to town for the wine tasting, I was laughing unconcernedly with him about the encounter. No more free macarons, he chortled.

Leaning our identical yellow bikes against the side alley of Aux vins de Malloren, Papaly went ahead of me to the garden in preparation. I took my time, making sure the wheels on my bike didn't crush the dandelions sprouting whimsically from the concrete foundation.

"Those are weeds, you know. You don't have to mind them. Saul will end up ripping them out, anyway."

Appoline appeared over my shoulder, smelling of mauve hand soap and buttery croissants. She was wearing mid-length khaki shorts and another oversized button-down. This one was shaded cream and looked much more worn. She had it tucked into her shorts, a brown belt tying the whole outfit together. Once again, she wore the collar loosely, gold chain tickling her sternum. Her wet hair was tied up, out of her face.

"Well." I licked my lips, trying to steal a taste of her scent. "Then Saul will have to rip them out, knowing someone else purposefully didn't."

Appoline rolled her eyes. "You speak so delicately. Not everything has to be poetry, Bellamy."

"*Pourquoi?*" *Why?* I let the word roll off my tongue. "Are riddles better?"

"*Non.* Because then you'd always have to wait for everyone's answers to things. I'm always hearing a collection of words strung together to sound smart, adequate, vindicated. You're allowed to just say things, you know. Scream, shout, spit. Who cares? There doesn't always have to be elegiac justice to what you do." She was out of breath after this rant. I raised my eyebrows at her.

"Elegiac?" I questioned.

"You're not the only one who reads. I managed to graduate high school," she said.

"Hey." She looked at me as I spoke now, slightly annoyed. "Saul is going to have to kick my ass to pull these flowers," I said.

We laughed together, full of existence, full of time. With her arm linked through mine, we cordially skipped to the back gardens of Aux vins de Malloren, where Papaly stood amidst excited tourists and leathery villagers, all drinking their mirth. Proudly, I watched as he'd speak with a customer, size them up, and then either pour them a glass of wine or fastidiously craft a cocktail of his own creation.

Saul, the owner, was running around the grounds excitedly. He was short, bald, and clearly elated at his booming business.

"Come, let's have him make us a drink." Appoline dragged me over to my grandpa.

"Don't you think it's a little early to be drinking?" I asked her.

"Look around, Bellamy. We're at a wine tasting. In France. Now answer that question yourself. Even the civilized drink wine."

Unable to argue with her logic, we walked over to Papaly, who was blushing with merriment. As I was about to introduce Appoline, the pair squealed with delight. My grandpa came around the tiny bar set under the willow tree and kissed her affectionately on both cheeks.

He held her hands tenderly, and I heard him say something about Appoline being his favorite customer. She returned the compliment, their rapport bouncing adoringly back and forth in winding French. I stood there, slightly confused and astounded that the two remembered each other, and were much less...friends?

"*C'est mon amie, Appoline.*" *It's my friend,* I said slowly to my grandpa.

He nodded eagerly.

"*Oui, oui, ma préférée!*" *His favorite,* he exclaimed.

Appoline smiled bashfully at me.

"*Tiens, tiens.*" Papaly ushered us to his cart of spirits and in moments had created a beautifully orange drink, sparkling with notes of honey. He handed it to Appoline, who smelled it, then took a sip, exclaiming with appreciation.

"*Oh là là! Bernard, j'aime ça!*" *I like this,* Appoline bellowed approvingly, gulping it down in indulgent sips as my grandpa beamed with satisfaction.

"*Et, pour ma belle petite fille.*" *And for my beautiful granddaughter.* Papaly handed me a fragile glass filled with a green liquid.

"*C'est quoi?*" I wasn't sure what he had given me.

As he spoke hurriedly in French, Appoline decided to translate for me.

"He said it's absinthe," she said lightly.

"Just, just absinthe?" I asked, vaguely disappointed he hadn't put as much thought and vigor into creating me a specialized drink, as he had for Appoline.

"He said its simplicity is misleading, because only rebels drink it and only rebels enjoy it...like you."

I scoffed when she said this.

"*Quoi?*" *What?* my grandfather inquired innocently, waiting patiently with large eyes, for me to take a sip.

Nervously, I pressed the glass to my lips, afraid I wouldn't like it. Surprisingly enough, it tasted like victory, like an insurgent on the brink of revolution, like a spiritually charged revelation. It was beautiful and emerald and with my grandpa waiting there, hands clasped, I knew I needed it.

"This fucking rocks." I burst.

All three of us laughed and clapped joyously.

"Now that, is poetry." Appoline squeezed my cheek, as did my grandpa.

Everyone was always squeezing them. We kissed Papaly goodbye and continued to walk around the garden, summer drinks clinking in hand.

With genuine interest and care, Appoline took her time to greet a handful of friends, friends of friends, and even tourists that she had met earlier that week. They all lined up and leaned in to give her fond kisses. Everyone gravitated toward her warmth. Her smile, so loud, yet approachable, summoned one particular woman who thanked her repeatedly for the extra room at her hotel. Apparently, the resort she had originally booked canceled on her at the last minute. By chance, Appoline had heard her crying and immediately offered her a stay at the Hôtel Alarie.

I was perplexed, but not surprised, at her kindness. She had always been a generous soul. It was just mesmerizing to watch this wild French girl, who'd slept on a dock the night before, drunk and unafraid, speak so eloquently with everyone and anyone around her. The charm she harnessed was her ability to be a nonconformist, yet make you feel welcomed and whole.

"So, are we going to talk about you calling my grandpa by his first name?" I teased once we slipped away to a less populated patch of greenery.

We sat underneath the shade of apple trees, leaves littering the crown of my head. Appoline pulled a few from my bun, blowing them into the courtyard. I wondered if she was making any wishes. At the time, I thought she just enjoyed watching the leaves somersault, gusts of wind pushing them left and right.

"I think that should be one of those things we just never talk about. We both know it happened, but we don't have to address it."

Winking, she swished back the rest of her drink and chewed nonchalantly on the ice.

"Appoline, until right now, I had forgotten my grandfather even had a first name."

Appoline took the glass out of my hand and gently tipped my chin back. While I stared upward at the ripening apples, robust with potential, she spoke steadily.

"Open," was her first command.

I parted my lips, no longer afraid to hesitate.

"Close your eyes," she was whispering now. She didn't touch me, but I could feel her skin next to mine. Entranced in the fantasy of fresh fruit and French tongues and open summers, I didn't flinch when she poured the absinthe in my mouth, not stopping until every drop was gone.

I heard her sigh. "I've been coming to these wine tastings every Saturday for two years. Your grandpa makes some damn good drinks, and I like his company. It took him about five months to start remembering me, but once he did, he looked out for me every week, a new drink always waiting."

I licked my lips, sticky with residue. "I'm glad he had you," I said, eyes still closed.

Guiltily, I realized the years I didn't come back, Appoline was here with him, being his friend.

"It's not as exciting as it could've been. Imagine if I were his long-lost granddaughter, or even his mistress!" she shrieked, full of longing and rosiness. Her eyes gleamed with lust.

"Who's the poet now?" I asked, lowering my chin and opening my eyes to look at her.

She was staring straight at me, on the verge of vulnerability. The trees rustled at this very moment, whispering secrets from limb to limb.

I remember the radio blaring from the bullhorn above the back entrance. It was the summer of Paul Simon. Sometimes, and in this instance, Art Garfunkel would make an appearance, singing over the scenes of my rather simple, yet intensely fervent vacation, coated with ravenous bites of sugary insight, ones that always left me thirsty.

The soundtrack to my summer stemmed solely from bullhorns and jukeboxes and the throaty hum of French villagers, all singing "Cecilia" as they bought cheese and butter in heavy troves from the market, where desire and passion and aching hunger were discovered. The orange glow of auburn light never ceased. The market was always burning, always satiating.

My sundress flared at the edges, as if perturbed by my grandfather, who was speaking daintily about me with a stranger and pointing in my direction. I swore loudly as the man turned, and I realized François had come looking for me. He looked innocent in a way that was neither charming nor reasonable for a man of his age and stature.

Nonetheless, his boyish dimples and delighted persistence drew me to him, like an owner finding her lost puppy, or a grandmother remembering her youth.

François wandered over to where Appoline and I sat. Neither of us had been able to speak, we were just indulging in the rounded space between us, or lack thereof.

"Uh, bonjour, Appoline. Bellamy." François was much more nervous outside the safety of his boulangerie.

Standing, we both greeted him, exchanging pleasantries, and of course, kisses.

"Your grandfather makes a delicious pastis," he said, holding up his drink as though we wouldn't have believed it otherwise.

"Wait," I stuttered. "You speak English?"

I had forgotten about formalities and caught myself fascinated with this world of sun-kissed gardens and people of language and blunt conversation.

"Oui. I was trying to tell you earlier this morning, but you ran out so quickly, I didn't have the chance." François' cheeks were stained with embarrassment.

"This morning...?" Appoline looked back and forth between François and I, clearly amused.

"It was nothing, I just spit up on him." I waved my hand capriciously, intrigued with his intent. I knew he enjoyed looking at me.

Eyes widened, Appoline smiled, relishing the tension. "Oh là là." She nudged François.

"It was the first time anyone has ever thrown up my black currant macarons, and in front of my mother, too!" he laughed.

I appreciated the repartee. "You should really watch where you're going. I could've choked and died. That's a lawsuit waiting to happen."

I reached at Appoline, trying to grab my glass back from her.

"It's empty," she said. She wouldn't let go of it.

"I would never let you die in my own store... I'd drag you outside, first." François joked.

He purposely took a swig of his drink and acknowledged Appoline holding mine with an unrelenting grip.

"How chivalrous." I crossed my arms over my chest.

The long sleeve I was wearing on top of my sundress didn't seem to cover me enough. I could feel the bareness of my breasts against the shirt, reflecting in his eyes.

"Don't worry, I know...um...CPR?" he said, finding humor within himself.

Appoline choked, and I was unsure if this was because he was beating her in her own game of blunt tête-à-tête, or if she was truly revolted at his poor attempt of seduction. I found their gentle rivalry oddly precious, two French people, beautiful with satin hair and licentious eyes, unaware that they were at odds with one another.

"Anyway, Bellamy, I was wondering if you would like to go out for dinner sometime. Your grandpa told me you enjoy gâteau Basque, and I know a place in town where they make the best ones."

He was growing more confident with every sip. Deciding to finish off the pastis made specifically for him, he turned to look at Appoline, smiling delicately.

"I figured since you're dating *mon ami*, us four could go out together, have a drink. It'd be a grand time," he continued.

Expectantly, he waited for her response. She squinted her eyes. "Why yes, François, it *would* be a grand time. But Carlo is out of town for the next week, you know this."

They both seemed to have forgotten I was standing there, silently watching them.

"Oh yes, that's right. Very well, Bellamy?" François was keen as he turned his eyes on me.

"Um, well, we could wait for...Carlo? To return?" I was caught in the ardor of it all, my head fluffy and light, begging to remember every imperative detail.

"Don't be silly, Bellamy. You should go. You'll have fun." Appoline had decided.

The three of us stood there, the turbulent and unforgiving sun forever beating down. François said tonight would be, unequivocally, the best night for a gâteau Basque. Allowing the fate of my summer to be tossed around, I agreed, miraculously tethered calmly to the ground.

After kissing us both faintly on the cheeks, François spun away, adamant about returning to the boulangerie. Swiftly, Appoline and I began to talk over one another, hearts racing with adrenaline.

"No, shut up, wait. You have a boyfriend?" I asked, perplexed she hadn't mentioned this earlier.

"*Bah, oui.* I have plenty," was her cheeky response.

"Do they all know about each other?"

"But of course!" She was appalled at my audacity to ask such a question.

"You're such a spiritual anarchist." I could feel the absinthe bubbling in my veins.

"*Non,* I'm just a whore." At that, she galloped away for a second drink, bought a large bottle of wine from an exuberant Saul, and insisted I have another glass of absinthe.

The air was feathery, wisps of shallow wind consistently tickling our faces. Overworked fishermen could be heard grunting from the sea, and I exulted in the dominance of antiquity that feasted over me. Many years before us, people had been here, drinking and living. And many years after us, they would continue to drink and live.

Appoline laughed me out of my serene consciousness. "Your daydreams are not conducive, Bellamy."

She pointed at my shoe, crushing the dandelions by my bicycle, the ones I had tried so hard to avoid damaging. Raising her eyebrows, she gave me a knowing look.

"Appoline," I said, caressing her chin in my hands and then mounting my bike. "Right now, I'm just drinking and living. Let's go."

She hopped on the back of my seat, hands on my shoulders. We rode from Aux vins de Malloren, past the boulangerie and the pub and the many women with small children, sand under their fingernails, dirty unwashed feet.

Chapter Seven

THE AFTERNOON WAS COMING to a regal end, the boats at shore and the people asunder. Appoline and I napped voraciously, consuming the space in my bed, entangled dreamily in the white cotton sheets.

I woke at around four, Appoline's hand pressed down on the hardened muscles in my back. Her eyelashes twitched tenderly, then settled on her cheeks. Quietly, I ran to the kitchen for a pitcher of water, drowning in thirst. My mom asked if Appoline would be staying for dinner, but I told her we had other plans for the night. She smiled and said she'd make two extra quiches, just in case.

Appoline was sitting, swanlike, in the center of my bed when I returned. She had the blanket twirled around her head.

"I woke up and you were gone," she yawned.

I held up the pitcher of water and she reached out, drinking straight from it, greedily.

"That was the best sleep I've gotten in months," Appoline said.

"You mean your bed of gold at Hôtel Alarie doesn't do it for you?" I winked this time.

"Gold beds aren't as soft as cotton ones."

Swiftly, I joined her under the blanket. We hid from the world here, in our threaded fort. I felt twelve again, giggling and squirming about, mouthing nonsensical jokes to one another. We shared memories of past joys and remarkable regrets. I finally asked her about Carlo, hoping she wouldn't lie to me under the safety of our secret fort.

"You'll like him," she said.

"How do you know I'll like him?" I asked, hunched over, holding the blanket above my head.

"You like everyone."

"No, I tolerate everyone. I tolerate everyone who likes you."

"Want to know a secret?" She had taken over my bed, sprawled out as if she slept there every night.

"Always."

"Carlo is the boy I always had a crush on when I was younger.

Remember my parents' friends who own the canoe shop next to the hotel? Well, Carlo is their son," she explained.

"Wait, that boy was sixteen when we were ten." I said, reminiscing on the many summers we spent hiding behind kayaks and boating equipment to catch a glimpse of him tying knots and stocking shelves.

"*You* were ten, *I* was twelve. Anyway, I had forgotten about him until I saw him again earlier this year, chatting with François in the boulangerie. It was easier than I thought, to get him into bed." She was looking very closely at me now, making sure I was listening. "The secret, Bellamy, is that it wasn't as good as I was hoping it would be, as I had expected it to be." She sighed and fell backward, the blanket covering her face completely.

"Which part?" I asked quietly, not wanting to sound too interested.

"The kiss, the first kiss. I had imagined it so many times in my head that the actual affair was just, anticlimactic. First kisses always are. That's the secret."

Sitting back up and shrugging, she continued. "But anyway, he's a nice guy. You'll like him."

"And...what about the others?" I grinned.

"They're all nice guys."

It wasn't until about five that Appoline realized I needed to start getting ready for my dinner with François.

"I have another secret," she said slyly to me, pulling out the bottle of wine she'd bought earlier.

"Drink half of this, and your date is bound to be ten times better than it would have been originally. Everything he says will be funny. No awkward tension."

"If I drink half of that, I won't even make it to dinner." I shook my head as Appoline popped the bottle and offered me the first swig. Relinquishing my timidity, I grabbed the bottle by the neck and drank until I could feel her approving eyes settle happily on my throat.

"I'm impressed with your selection of wine. It makes me pucker with...gluttony?" I questioned myself. "Self-indulgence?"

"Only the best from Aux vins de Malloren." Appoline said sincerely.

"Named after my grandmother, you know."

Cherry stains of satin grapes covered my lips. Brushing them lightly with her thumb, Appoline quickly turned to my closet.

"I know, your grandfather told me," she said, her words muffled from the condensed air, humid and unkempt in the rear of the closet.

"Okay, seriously, next time just pretend you didn't know."

I was sitting at the boudoir mirror, disparaging my reflection for its youth. I didn't know it then, but Appoline saw Jean-Marc's sweater hidden near my suitcase that night, and she never said anything about it. I believe it might've been her way of allowing me to hold on to the memories of the future we had always longed for.

We took turns taking swigs from the ridiculously large bottle of wine, as Appoline did my makeup, applying rouge to my cheeks and eyelids. She reapplied the deep maroon shade to my lips over and over again, claiming it needed to be darker.

"I don't mind," I slipped. "Your fingers feel nice."

The record player in the corner of the room sprang dust and perpetual ramblings of "You Can Call Me Al" until we were too dizzy from all the excitement to play it over again. Exhausted and frustrated with my lack of sexy dresses and lacy bras, Appoline lay freely on my bed, feet in the air. She suddenly stood up and pointed at me.

"You're trying too hard. This isn't an infinite romance, it's a dinner. You might have sex, you might throw up on him again, but stop trying to make it so breathable. Who cares? It's just food."

I laughed candidly, caught off guard. She chuckled, took a sip of the wine, and jumped behind me. I twirled around, wearing a silky slip that could have been a nightgown.

"Getting dressed up is such a hassle." I sighed.

I jumped out my bay window that night, my knees itchy from the rose lotion I'd found underneath the sink and a mix of scented perfumes congealed in my hair, which was pulled up into a loose bun for continuity. Drunk from half a bottle of wine and flushed with uneasy excitement, I hugged Appoline quickly. She stared at me, her hands on my shoulders.

"*Tu es très belle.*" *You are very beautiful.*

I wasn't sure if her eyes were glistening or if the faint reverberance of the moon was sparkling from her irises.

"Wish me luck, *ma chérie.*" I winked at her and ran off toward town, forcing her to watch me leave in a spirited skip, the same way I had always watched her saunter off to her next engagement.

I wore a dark jean jacket atop my grey dress, glossy amongst the sultry fog. The evening air was gloomy, and I knew I looked quite dramatic waiting for François outside his boulangerie. Winged eyeliner traced my face, a vivid study of supermodels and immaculate imitation.

Once François locked the store, he walked over to where I was leaning with my leg wrapped around a streetlamp. He smiled, dimples carved into his cheeks. When he stretched out his hand, I thought he was looking for mine. Instead, he opened his palm. One beautifully opaque macaron sat there, pristinely.

"A little good luck snack, before we eat. I figured you didn't get to enjoy the ones you bought earlier this morning."

When he spoke, my stomach lurched. I had no choice but to be enthralled with his buoyancy.

I felt as though we could float along the cobbled roads for hours, just from the streaming current in his words. Taking the macaron, I split it in two, offering him the other half. This seemed to allure him, as he ate it in one bite, sucking on his fingers with an increased charisma.

The glamour of anticipation and unease serenaded us through the dwindling market and up toward the raging cliffs. Painted notes of crushed footpaths and ivory stars manicured the ambience of the evening. At the top of a particularly rigid bluff, François paused and set down the basket he had been carrying.

"This is it. We're here."

He stretched his arms, inviting the open expanse in for a salty embrace. As the torrent of waves and wind prickled my ankles, I held the skirt of my nightgown down, remembering I was bare beneath it.

I had been complaining that I didn't have any cute underwear, so Appoline told me not to wear any at all. She worked like that, in extremes. Nothing was ever too concerning for her; she always found a reason to push boundaries and deny limits. Excess was never out of reach.

François and I sat, overlooking the dark waters. The blanket he had brought for us to sit on was so soft, it took everything in me not to strip right then and there. I wanted to be engulfed by the relentless dream of sugary air.

We ate flatbread from the pizzeria that was adjacent to the barbershop where François said all the older gentlemen in town went just to complain about the diminishing fish in the sea. If a haircut came from the visit, then so be it, he said, but that was never the initial intent. I laughed, absorbed in his view of the village he'd lived in his whole life.

François explained that, originally, he'd wanted to go to university, but his father died, leaving his mother to man the boulangerie on her own. Not wanting the fate of their treasured bakery to fall within the curtain of his aging mother's responsibility, he stayed home.

He grew fond of it, he said, so he never left. Between gluttonous bites of tomato and mozzarella, I nodded and grunted, much like my grandfather. There wasn't much space for me to talk, but I didn't mind. Sometimes, I found peace in listening to others ramble passionately. It was beautiful. François wandered on and on, getting deeper and farther into his life, his past. He only stopped speaking once, in awe of how much pizza I had eaten.

"I'm a voracious eater." I stifled my words, thick from a full mouth. "You have to force me to stop eating, otherwise I might never quit."

"It's that good, huh?" he asked. "Well, don't get too full."

Pulling out the last items from the basket, he grinned widely. A gâteau Basque and a bottle of champagne graced the blanket between us.

"I don't get full." I pointed out before clapping at the spread before me. "What flavor?"

"Black cherry." François said, knowingly. "That's the one your grandpa came in and bought the first day you were here."

"Where's it from? You said it's the best one in town."

"I'd be a fool not to bring my own, then. Right?"

Slyly, he cut me a piece and I humored us both by picking it up with my hands and swallowing it whole. Admiration surrounded the night, following our footsteps and chasing us down to the beach. It was here that I stopped François, momentarily, and pointed out at the impenetrable skyline.

"I wish I was part of the sea," I murmured softly, quite at risk now of feeling the full effects of fermented grapes and flimsy innocence.

"I like being on solid ground." François stamped his foot. "The sea moves too much."

As I spun magically everywhere, the sand raining from the ground, I remembered why my bag was so heavy.

"Oh," I stopped, teetering slightly, and pulled out a fresh linen shirt, blue stripes lining the collar and cuffs. "I got this for you. I feel bad that I ruined your other one."

François was still, forcing me to walk toward him. He read the small note I had pinned to the shirt, out loud.

"I'm sorry I threw up on you...Bellamy."

Laughing jubilantly, he held the shirt to his chest. "You're quite the writer, aren't you? Honestly, how does it look? Are the stripes too much?"

"If the stripes were too much, I would've picked a different shirt." I smiled at him, still tiptoeing airily down the great divide, where ocean meets land.

"Thank you. I can't wait to wear it."

"I stole it from my grandpa's closet, so make sure to thank him, too." I said, jumping as small roves of waves chased my ankles up the shore.

Hurrying after me, François outran the rushing water, stopping me in my tracks.

"I enjoy your company," he stated with confidence.

"How old are you?" I asked.

"Thirty-six," he answered, not returning the question.

François bent down. He let the water pool in his hands, then flicked the remnants on my face.

"Okay. You're not too old to race me." I decided.

Partly because the wind was gathering speed and partly because my thoughts were taking an unprecedented existential turn as we lingered on the darkening beach, I sprinted away from shore, up toward the chattering cottages.

For a moment, I wasn't sure François would follow. I turned my head and saw him, unafraid of the daunting mass of thoughts I'd left behind to drift away on the ever-moving sea.

Overcome with fits of shrieking laughter, the two of us made our way carelessly to my cottage. As we finally caught our breath, François tripped, and I burst out laughing painfully once again.

"Are you afraid of me?" he asked suddenly, snickering.

His words were like a knife against the grain of calm that was settling in.

"I'm not afraid of anything, François."

My chest had settled to an even pace. We spoke in between the rock outlines set out front by my grandfather.

"It's just, most women don't run away from me during a romantic, long walk on the beach," he said.

"Most women probably wish they had." Channeling Appoline's adoration for banter, I suppressed the urge to wink. "I had a splendid evening."

"Oh? Did you?" François was smiling cheekily now. He inched his way toward me, smelling of sandalwood and desire.

"I didn't throw up on anyone, so I'd say it was a success."

"And I got a brand-new shirt out of it," he smiled smugly.

Holding up the collared chemise, we both stared at it, silent.

"Thanks for everything." I said politely, unaware how to bid him adieu and slip into the caress of my bedroom.

Placing his hands tenderly on my hipbones, he pulled me in and kissed me on each cheek. He stood tall against my frame, strong in his movements.

"Goodnight, Bellamy." François turned and walked past the collection of stones, a shadowy sum of the finest men in France, the ones I didn't crave enough.

Chapter Eight

STEEPING POMEGRANATE TEA AND arduous knitting lessons molded the mornings I spent letting my mother and grandfather keep me company. After I admitted to Papaly about stealing his shirt and giving it to François, he gave me two outstanding options: either ask for the shirt back or invite the baker over for dinner.

Excited with the prospect of filling Papaly's tiny home with young and lively guests, my mom suggested I invite Appoline as well, enthralling my grandfather, who promptly left to buy overpriced spirits for the occasion.

Gilded with sunlight, I rode my bike up the hills into the tourism district. It wasn't often I ventured over the bluffs to tinsel town. When I did, it was almost always certain that I wouldn't be able to find Appoline. She preferred the lackadaisical nature of the worn cottages and small market below, creating her own chaos amongst the perpetual calm. The birds were too prim here, she had once told me. It didn't feel natural for birds to have manners.

At the entrance to the Hôtel Alarie, I parked the chipped yellow bike neatly in the rack and smoothed my fleece shirt over my matching fleece shorts. The lobby was just as grand as I had remembered, full of sparkling marble and opal accents.

At the reception desk, I bounded back and forth with a confused old lady, her hair full of gossip and uncouth judgments. I tried to explain that Appoline was a friend of mine, but Muriel wouldn't hear of it, claiming Appoline was around somewhere, floating between "her many friends, many of which she didn't need, you know?"

I wasn't sure, but Muriel seemed to have an oddly large soft spot for Appoline, almost as if she were afraid that I was going to corrupt her.

As our conversing became irritant and Muriel was ready to run me out into the streets, I noticed a tiny Filipina woman scurrying behind the counter.

"Madame Alarie!" I exclaimed, nearly jumping over the desk and giving Muriel a heart attack.

Madame Alarie, as stated before, was a proper, brisk, and tiny woman of immense power. She'd met Monsieur Alarie when he was on a business trip in Rhode Island, and promptly moved to France with him upon his return. Their marriage of twenty-five years stood only to prove that Madame Alarie was able to keep the things she wanted, despite Monsieur Alarie's remarkably unfavorable family, who happened to loathe anyone who came between them and the prowess of their finances.

Turning abruptly, Madame Alarie greeted me with a quick and stale kiss, jumpy as usual. She made me promise that it was my grandfather who had been buying all the gâteaux Basque and not anyone else.

After repeatedly assuring her that it was my family with the affinity for gâteau Basque, she continued on, in English for both mine and Muriel's sake (the woman's hair was stuffed with secrets).

"And your grandpa is the one buying threes of everything? Everywhere I turn, three croissants are missing, three fresh baguettes...why this morning three bouquets of irises were gone from the florist, and yes, I know this because yesterday I went to scout some summer plants for the garden and there were only five bouquets of irises left and I knew I should've bought them then, but I figured they'd be there today. Well, they're not! The things I need are always gone." She looked at me, out of breath, waiting for a response.

I laughed affectionately. "No, no. We only buy hordes of food, not flowers," I said.

"I wasn't always like this, you know, but the moment you let your guard down, someone else has the things you need," she huffed.

Unsure how to bridge the gap, we both sighed, Madame Alarie, out of distress, and I, out of uncertainty.

"Will—will you let Appoline know she's invited to dinner at my grandpa's tonight? He's going to make cocktails. My mom is cooking a cassoulet, and I think we might even have a game of *pétanque* in the backyard. You're welcome to come as well."

Looking at her with timid eyes, I absorbed her light smile as she patted me on the shoulder.

"You were always my favorite friend of Appoline's. I think her favorite too. I'll let her know. What time?"

She gave Muriel a look as she grunted by the phonebook. I told Madame Alarie that dinner was at seven-thirty sharp and sprinted out of the lobby before anyone could say they ever saw me there, leaving coarse pieces of fleece to litter the marbled floors.

//

There was a church in town, just one. It knelt, glorified, on the steep of the longest cliff in Saint __ de Vie. I ran here for the first time, on that sweltering afternoon, afraid I'd forgotten what cathedral bells sounded like.

Caught in the rafters of the surging trees nestled primly together in the furthest stretch of secluded overhangs that dotted the church garden, I dangled upside down. Lazily, I ate an apple, scraping the skin with my thumb, letting the blood rush to my head.

The surging red in my eyes painted the town with scalding fire. I was supposed to be on my way to invite François to dinner, yet this was the first moment I felt I had supremely to myself. Melancholic anonymity shifted upward. I walked from limb to limb, suppressing myself from myself.

Ardent birds flew in between my arms, above and below me, unaware I was even there. I felt distant from all that I had and all that I was and all that I wanted. This stupor of nature's quelling silence completed my understanding that everything just came to be. I saw a priest cross the lawns. He smiled at me, cheerily, and continued on, unbothered by my presence, just like the birds.

//

When I invited François over for dinner, he was bashful, then upset I hadn't told him about this prestigious event earlier. How was he supposed to bake something special in this time frame? He wanted to know if I had an answer for him.

"Just bring something already baked." I squeezed his shoulder affectionately before walking back to the cottage, the moon just an outline in the sky, waiting for her turn to shine.

Papaly was pink with excitement. He wore his best sweater vest, brilliantly knitted colors spilling together at the seams. On the kitchen counter, he had nine different types of liquor, four bottles of wine, and an abundance of ripening fruit laid out on display. My mom was enjoying a petite glass of wine as she waited on her cassoulet to finish baking. I pranced around the dining room, simply because that's what you do when music is playing.

At seven-twenty-five, Appoline rapped on the front door, stirring my surprise as she was never on time for anything, much less early. We hadn't spoken since my date with François a few evenings before, so I expected her to bury me with questions. Instead, she kissed me on both cheeks and asked me where my grandfather was.

"My mom made biko," she said. "It's a Filipino dessert."

"Where is she tonight?" my mom asked, giving Appoline a warm hug.

"She's doing a sweep of the hotel; she likes to work late some nights."

"Well, it's great to have you here, sweetie." My mom pinched her cheek and ogled at the biko.

Papaly hurrahed at Appoline's presence and made her a drink. This one was much darker and heavier than the one he'd made her at the wine tasting. He said her mood was denser and more solidified today.

As Appoline chatted with my mom and grandfather, I stood in the nook, patiently watching. Sometimes I felt as though I were merely in the audience of her life, watching as she made everything into a movie. Spirited or not, it was a performance, nonetheless. I don't think she knew how to act, steady or calm, unless it was for others.

François showed up a few minutes later, right on time, carrying a bouquet of flourishing irises.

"Where did you get those?" I asked, wide eyed and slightly nervous, for his sake.

"At the florist..." His voice trailed off as Appoline rounded the corner.

"Oh, you're going to be in so much trouble with my mom," she teased.

My mom and grandfather now stood behind Appoline, curiously waiting for us three to make our way to the kitchen. François' eyes lit up as he handed my mom the bouquet of flowers.

"François," I said, trying to break the ice. "You wouldn't happen to have bought any other bouquets of irises, would you?"

"Actually, funny you should ask. I bought two more for the bakery windows. They were just so beautiful; I couldn't resist."

He scanned the room, unaware that Appoline and I were trying to hold in our laughter, until eventually our bellies burst, and my mother shushed me for being impolite.

Once Papaly had made each of us a drink and was confident he had pinpointed all of our moods (each of which apparently were begging to be satiated), we sat around the table, cassoulet warm in the center.

We were a passively aggressive, yet calm cluster that night. A group of Frenchmen eyeing the dinner, as a passionate desire for exuberant conversation and undetectable competition resonated between us.

On one end, Papaly sat knife and fork in hand, handkerchief neatly folded on his lap. He was milking a tiny glass of whiskey and kept his back against the line of liquor behind him. The *"Roi du Vin."* We petitioned the wine king whenever we wanted another drink. Appoline found great amusement in this, therefore, so did François.

On the other end of the table, my mom sat, indulging both of our guests in amiable French conversation, leaving me to eavesdrop and interpret at my own pace. I didn't mind being left out. It gave me time to eat my cassoulet and enjoy the show. Mother drank a mauve brandy and couldn't resist puckering at each sip.

Across from me, Appoline and François were comfortable and keen in my grandfather's velvet chairs that he had brought out from storage specifically for the occasion. They ate and laughed and demanded drinks from *le Roi du Vin* all throughout dinner, much to his delight.

At one point, we played a heated game of musical chairs, except we all passed our drinks around the table, sampling each one. Papaly played Jean-Jacques Goldman's *"Je te donne"* and every time he sang, *'je te donne,'* we stopped and took a sip of whatever drink was in our hand.

This led to shouts across the table like, "So this is what Bellamy tastes like," and "Wow, Papaly, you think Appoline is sad, huh? This one's strong!"

"François, you're drinking this? When did you become so sensitive?" I shouted, one of the many digs.

At one point, Appoline ended up with two drinks in her possession just as Jean-Jacques Goldman was repeating *'je te donne.'*

Remembering that I was apparently a rebel in secret, I dared her to chug them both. François and my mom joined in, all of us chanting and banging our fists on the table.

"Chug! Chug! Chug!"

We shouted gleefully, red in the face and mushy in our stomachs from the cassoulet, glued to our intestines like concrete. Papaly, who didn't understand what was happening or what we were saying, took to the bar once again, and used his fingers to conduct our chants as if we were a finely tuned, drunken orchestra.

Seeing this, Appoline gave in and stood up. We all quieted, waiting with apprehension. Then, she raised both glasses, and we heckled her from the crowded dining room table.

"Je te donne!" she exclaimed before downing both mine and François' drinks.

We all clapped, egging her on, and Papaly danced around the table, handing out more drinks to those who had either finished or lost theirs to Appoline.

"Oh, *non*." François wagged his finger and joked about being called sensitive.

He refused to drink the light, buttery-colored cocktail set before him. My grandpa grunted and put his hands on his hips. François pointed at me and Papaly argued back, the two steadily disagreeing in lighthearted banter. Finally, Papaly gave up, threw his hands in the air, then took the drink and downed it all in one swallow.

"Papa! Qu'est-ce que tu fais? Merde!" What are you doing? My mom spit out her chardonnay and stood up.

Papaly explained he was showing François how to be a real man. All of us sat, teetering, tottering, and hollering with laughter. After this, Papaly served each of us a glass of cognac, explaining we were all 'men' now.

Simultaneously, the five of us sipped the brandy, old-fashioned-stare-down style. Silent and eyes squinting, we watched one another, waiting to ruthlessly point out the chump who couldn't handle their liquor.

After what seemed like an eternity, François' eye twitched and it was all over.

"GOOSE!" I yelled accusingly, pointing my finger at him.

Everyone followed my lead, and François covered his face in playful embarrassment.

"Wait...goose?" Appoline questioned.

I shrugged. "We're drunk. Drunk, drunk...goose?"

Somehow, she accepted this explanation, and only a little while later, the lively dinner party had turned to a quaint parlor filled with handsome people, slipping between the hazy pull of sleep and the desperate ache of engaged presence.

Appoline was the first to leave. She was clothed in a gentle intoxication and let the seaside breeze cool her puffy face. After thanking Papaly and my mother for a marvelous evening and declining my offer to spend the night, she walked with me to the front door.

Insisting that she was off to meet Carlo, she kissed me on the cheeks and nodded knowingly behind me, where François was waiting.

"*Bisous*," she said.

And off she went, skipping down the stone-lined path and into the wash of trees, a couple of irises she had stolen from François' bouquet tucked behind her ear.

François was next to bid his adieu. Embracing me with a quiet lust that I could feel emanating from his chest, he whispered goodnight and assured me that he'd catch up to Appoline and make sure she got to her next destination safely. Off he went. Destination? I thought. Where was she destined to end up tonight, after filling our home with so much life? Where was she taking whatever remained of her spirit? Where would she leave parts of herself tonight, to be forgotten and uncared for in the morning?

I walked languidly to where my mother sat on the marmalade couch, knitting slowly. Papaly kissed me on the forehead and squeezed my mom's shoulder before heading off to bed. The front windows swayed ominously, back and forth on their hinges, allowing the sea to engulf our lonely leftovers and spilled spirits.

"I'm sad," I said.

My mom hesitated with the needles for a brief second, but continued knitting, not breaking her stride.

"I know, *mon bébé*."

"You know?" I asked.

I sat next to her, legs crossed on the couch, a pillow in my lap as my buffer.

"More often than not, we're sad. When the happiest of moments pass, we're just reminded of that."

"This evening was happy," I stated.

"Yes, so tonight, you'll feel even sadder."

She sighed, and I knew she knew. She wasn't sure, but she knew. I lay my head on her lap, and she set her knitted blanket across my face and laughed.

"Well, at least we can keep your face warm." She cradled my head in her hands. "It's perfect."

Sighing, I fell asleep for a few sweet moments, before awaking groggily and walking to my bed, where I slept lavishly in my beautiful divan of cotton sheets and lavender dreams.

My mom must not have gone to bed that night. The next morning, I found her asleep on the couch, the foot-long piece of fabric she had been working on splayed across her chest, keeping her just warm enough.

Chapter Nine

IT TOOK ME A few days to recover from the hangover I had following our lavish dinner party. Thankfully, Appoline dropped by multiple times, bringing us more biko since her mom had made too much and didn't know what to do with it all. I lay in bed, covered in a brown sugar and coconut milk glaze, positive Appoline's skin tasted just as sweet.

I hadn't moved from my room for a few days, unsure why I was feeling so melancholic, and had decided I'd stay there until I could figure it out. I was missing home and the indifference to all I felt there. I craved the safety of freshly mown lawns and severe suburbia.

Three days into my extreme, piteous self-loathing, Appoline forced me out of bed with the promise of more biko. This time, I had to eat it on the beach though, that was her only condition.

"Ugh," I complained. "Don't you just want to hang out here, eat, and relax?"

"What have I created?" she muttered. "No more biko. No. Not unless you get up and eat it on the beach with me. Have you even been to the beach yet? Have you put on a swimsuit one time since you've been here?"

"Ouch. No need to call me out like that. I'm eating biko. I can't wear a swimsuit. The two are mutually exclusive. You should know this."

I wrapped a bedsheet around my head, frowning at her.

"Not a single thing in this world is mutually exclusive with another," she said promptly, her eyes wide.

In one hand, she held a plate of biko and in the other, she held a swimsuit.

"Fine. I eat, you swim," I said.

"*Bah, non. Absolument pas.*"

Appoline threw the swimsuit at my face. Five minutes later, we were walking down the sloping beach, a giant sweatshirt covering my bikini, as well as my shame.

"Since when did you start watching baseball...and supporting the Marlins? That's obscure." I questioned, beginning to sweat in my ridiculous outfit.

Appoline walked a few steps ahead, her one-piece swimsuit slightly damp against her skin. She wore a pair of loose jeans, unbuttoned at the waist, and a Marlins baseball cap on top of her long, braided hair that trailed down her back.

"It's Carlo's hat," she shrugged.

"Ah. Hey, how was the other night with him? He's been back awhile, and you still haven't introduced me to him."

I was as cool and casual as I could possibly be, all the while trying to evade heat stroke.

"You've been avoiding me just to hang with him." I accused her.

"I haven't been avoiding you to spend time with him, I've been avoiding you to give you time to spend with François. I'm a thoughtful friend," she said.

"I don't need any time alone with François," I said disdainfully, tightening the hood of my sweater around my face.

"Oh, yeah you do," she teased.

"Oh yeah? Why's that?"

Appoline walked over to me, and after a short fight, pulled open my hood.

"The sun! You need it. Stop with your nonsense, Bellamy, I swear, sometimes I think you enjoy being reproachful."

"That's entirely untrue. I'm a very pleasant person, a poetic one even, at times." I stood there in the midafternoon heat, bundled up, with my arms crossed.

"François likes you. He told me after we left your house the other night." Appoline said this bluntly and continued to make her way toward shore.

"Well, has anyone bothered to ask me if I like him?" I stood still, unmoving. She turned around, saw me, and grunted loudly before charging at me.

"I'm tired of this! Take it off!" Appoline lifted my arms and wrenched the giant sweatshirt over my head.

Surprised she got it off so easily, she looked at me, looked back at the sweatshirt, then chucked it over my head up the sandy dune. I stood there, slightly disconcerted but not stunned, hunched over in my brown-fringed bikini.

Calmly, I said, "Do you feel better now?"

Appoline breathed heavily and stepped closely to me.

"*Oui*," she said, looking me deeply in the eyes, hardened and annoyed. She began to walk away, and I grabbed her arm, pulling her back so she could feel my intensity.

"If François likes me so much, why hasn't he kissed me yet?" I asked.

I knew she could taste my breath, just inches from the invisible line that separated our noses from touching. She pulled away again and this time I let her. Walking down the beach, I followed.

"What do you mean he hasn't kissed you?" She wouldn't face me, but instead looked around and decided now was the time to take her pants off and set up camp.

"He hasn't kissed me. He's had many chances, but just hasn't done it," I said as I watched Appoline lay her jeans out on the sand and rest promptly on top of them. "Fuck, we didn't bring towels." Before Appoline could make a snarky response, I added, "It's fine, I'll just sit in the sand and become one with Mother fucking Earth. I'm being pleasant!"

"Maybe he's nervous," Appoline suggested, shading her eyes from the sun with her hand.

"He's thirty-six. Did you know that? Men of that age don't get nervous. I can't figure him out. How can I tell the difference between a friendly kiss on the cheek and an...amorous one?" I asked, sitting fist deep in the scalding grains of sand.

Appoline laughed.

"Amorous? You mean romantic?" she asked.

"No, I mean sensual." I was feeling rather persnickety and wanted explicit answers.

Sitting up, Appoline brushed sand off her tanned back.

"The French in you is really coming out," she said, impressed.

"It's just, he always pulls me close, I can feel his heart beating, and I think he's going in for a *real* kiss, and then...cheek kiss. All of France gives me those kisses. My cheeks will be chapped by the time I leave." I had dug my palms so far into the sand, I was elbow deep.

"Cheek kisses *are* real kisses, Bellamy," Appoline insisted.

"In theory, yes, but they're not kisses that differ any from my grandfather's."

I was adamant about this.

"Well, come here. How do you know his cheek kisses aren't sensual? They could be. It all depends on his technique."

Appoline motioned for me to come closer. I looked at her, then back at my arms, halfway to the lava underground. She rolled her eyes and sat across from me.

"Okay, kiss me goodnight the way he kisses you goodnight."

Appoline leaned in, letting her cheeks rest in front of mine. I laughed uneasily.

"This is classic. Don't use this as an excuse to actually kiss me, Appoline," I said, unsure where all this confidence had arisen from and unsure why it had arisen now.

Appoline blushed briefly, then waved it off.

"You would like it," she joked, much lighter and easier than I had. "Come now, show me how he does it."

Hands still grasping at the earth's core, I leaned forward and swiftly kissed each one of her cheeks. I did this quickly, unable to even fully remember what François' lips felt like against the apples of my cheeks. Appoline shook her head.

"No." She leaned forward and grazed each cheek against each cheek of mine. "Did he do it like that? Or..." Her voice trailed off as she went back to my cheeks, pressing her red lips against each one, softly, but with intent. "Did he do it like that?" She faced me. I could feel the sun browning my neck from behind.

"What's the difference?" I asked, staring right at her, oblivious.

She laughed wholly and nudged my shoulder.

"See, the first one is what all of our aunts and uncles and grandparents do. They quickly press their cheeks to ours, making a kissing noise. It's much less intimate this way, but it still plays off as a kiss. The second one, where lips meet cheek, is when you know things are dear and burning between you two."

Again, she shrugged and laid back down on her jeans.

"Well, that's annoying," I said.

"Why?" Appoline kicked her feet in the air.

"Because I can't remember which one François always gives me."

We both laughed.

"It's like that sometimes, huh? We're so caught up in the moment—" Appoline began.

"That you forget to notice the details," I finished.

"Exactly! Half the time, I don't even remember what Carlo and I do, I just focus on how it makes me feel," she admitted lightly.

"And how does this amazing Carlo make you feel?" I teased her with enough interest to beckon an answer from her quickly and truthfully.

"Wanted, I guess. Yeah, he makes me feel wanted."

Appoline and I lounged on the sandy beach, away from the tourists and the ice cream vendors. Only the boats could be seen, bobbing in the waving distance. After thirty minutes of tanning in the blistering and ungodly sun, Appoline let me eat the rest of the biko, as a treat.

I remember some of that sugared glaze dripped down onto my sternum. I was always a messy eater. Appoline used her forefinger to wipe it away, tasting it.

"Mmm. Sweet," she said.

"You didn't eat any..." I said, realizing Appoline hadn't eaten any biko while she was with me. "Hey, you didn't eat much the other evening at dinner. I'm just realizing..."

But Appoline cut me off. "I'm never hungry when I'm with you," she said as matter of fact, and raced to the waves.

After this inexplicable statement, we splashed in the water singing, "Je te donne," living in the memory from nights before.

"Hey, who am I?" I splashed over to her and nuzzled my cheeks embarrassingly against hers. She laughed and splashed water at me.

"François! Get away from me! I'm going to tell Bellamy!" she shrieked.

As we dried off, I ran around the beach with no inhibitions, searching for the sweatshirt Appoline had angrily discarded off my back earlier. I found it lying just feet from the sidewalk. As I waited for Appoline to reach me, the butt of her jeans wet from her swimsuit, I reveled in the glory of summer days and best friends.

I smiled and stopped smiling and smiled some more. She was dancing up the dune, licking the rest of the glaze from the empty container.

"Hey," she said once she was able to walk in stride with me, her arm around my waist.

"Hey," I said back.

"You do like him though, right?" she asked.

"Yeah...I like him," I agreed.

Appoline turned to face me and grabbed both of my hands.

"Good," she beamed. "Tonight you, me, Carlo, and François are going out!" She paused, giving me a sly look. "Make sure to moisturize your cheeks!"

With this, she raised her eyebrows, laughed, and sprinted toward my grandpa's cottage.

"Dibs on the shower! I have dibs on the shower!" I yelled, running after her, knowing very well I'd never catch up.

As we approached the cottage, we saw Papaly out front, adding more stones to his collection of the outlined path. He wore a large-brimmed sun hat and gardening gloves as he kneeled next to the petunias. Appoline watched him as if she wanted to say something, but decided against it. He waved to us as we passed by. Inside, my mother was in the kitchen nook, knitting. The house smelled warm. Rosemary and oregano drifted melodiously through the living room.

Appoline and I retreated to my bedroom, aware the afternoon was on its final lingering stretch.

"Shoot, I told Carlo and François we'd meet them at the dock around four," Appoline said, tapping the wooden clock above the dresser.

"You told them this before you even asked me if I wanted to go. What would you have done if I had said no?" I asked.

"I would've gone on a date with two boys. It's not anything I haven't done before." She winked at me, and for the first time, I felt uneasy.

"Come on." She grabbed my arm and pushed me into the shower. "Let's just both shower really quick so we can save time."

Warm droplets sprinkled across my face as I stood behind Appoline, her back stooped, hands cupping the rushing torrent of water in front of her. She had pulled her swimsuit down. It hung, stretched tightly against her waist. Lines of bronzed skin laced her shoulders, revealing the lighter virgin skin that had never seen sun.

With the bar of lavender and chamomile soap, she scrubbed her body, never turning away from the water, never facing me. I waited patiently, allowing the leftover spray from her private shower to dampen my skin. Over her shoulder, she passed me the soap. Frothy bubbles swam adoringly down her spine and into the bottom half of her swimsuit.

Lathering her arms and legs, she rinsed off, letting the shower stream run down her front. I stared, almost feeling foul, as if I were spying on an intimate moment, yet I couldn't look away. I accidentally noticed the rounded edges of her breasts spilling lightly over her side and my throat suddenly felt dry, despite the crashing throes of water around me.

"Thanks for letting me go first," Appoline said.

She slipped out of the shower, her tangle of blackened hair sweeping past my chin and reminding me what it felt like to be awoken from a daydream. I didn't want her to go, but I was glad to have the shower to myself so she couldn't feel my anxiety heating the space between us.

Brushing my chin and trying not to sneeze from the tickle, I grunted and stepped forward, now allowing the entire jet of ceaseless water to pummel my body and wash away my sins.

Emerging from the steamed bathroom, refreshed and sparkling with dew, I decided to walk straight to my closet, bare. Appoline didn't realize it, but she had taken the last clean towel. She was kneeling on my bed, her elbows on the bay window behind the pillows, looking past the array of trees and bushes in the garden.

I crossed the room, creaking wood panels narrating my every step. Looking at the clothes that littered my wardrobe, I knew half my silhouette could be seen, if one were to peek past the doorway. Though I never saw her turn her head, I know she looked. Neither of us said a word. It seemed we were playing a game, but I wasn't sure who was winning and what it would feel like to lose.

Thirty minutes later, we were dressed, poised and unstoppable. Appoline sported a blue, silky button-down long sleeve that she wore pretentiously undone and widely open. She told me the wind would be her accessory this evening. Her dark-washed denim jeans were loose, yet they enhanced her figure with the effect of mysterious curiosity. Appoline was a fucking powerhouse.

I stood next to her, feeling equally as confident. Once you've showered with someone, your insecurities either intensify or just peacefully slip away. I think she felt this way, too. We were at ease. I wore a tight black turtleneck that cut off just below my bellybutton, the fabric skimming my skin with each twist and turn. The black jean shorts Appoline gave me to wear covered my hips with passion.

"Bravo!" Papaly shouted.

My mom took our picture, the only one we got all summer, and off we went to meet the French boys at the dock.

Carlo jumped into the sea when he saw Appoline. From afar, we saw him and François talking and shuffling their feet lazily as they waited for us.

"*Bonjour, mes chéris!*" Appoline called from the umbrella stand toward the rear of the dock.

Promptly and with no hesitation, Carlo kissed his fingers and did a backflip off the edge of the wharf, making waves that the ocean hadn't seen since 1974. That was the year a group of fishermen had caught a baby whale, accidentally rousing the entire ecosystem below the earth.

The media had then since declared Saint __ de Vie the Town of Whales, which actually caused some controversy between the idyllic seaside village and the country of Wales, who accused France of attempting to profit off their namesake.

Naturally, after Carlo jumped, the two of us rushed toward François, who was laughing, full of amusement. In French, Appoline yelled at him, asking what the hell was going on. François hugged us both as we searched for Carlo amongst the watery carnage.

"Oh, look!" François pointed to somewhere in the distance.

As all three of us squinted, he wrapped his arms around our waists and pulled us close. Seconds later, he had dragged us against our will, into the ocean with him. We were swimming unevenly amongst the fish in the sea, kicking and splashing. François floated on his back, laughing at our shrieks.

"It hasn't even been five minutes on this date, and my hair is already ruined." I said, treading water, not necessarily bothered.

"That's quite a statement." François flicked some water at my nose. "A date, ooooo."

"Well, that's what this is, isn't it?" Now that I was soaking wet and splashing in the waves, it didn't seem like façades were necessary.

"We might as well be transparent with one another," I said, and nodded at his shirt.

He was wearing the white collared shirt with thin blue lines that I had gifted him. It was now completely translucent, plastered to his skin from the current.

"Oh, how embarrassing," he joked. "You look beautiful by the way."

"Next time, tell me that before you push me into the ocean, because now I know it's a lie."

I swam away, diving toward seaweed clusters and floating baubles of sand that generously moved aside for my schoolgirl butterfly stroke.

Next to me, I saw Appoline scolding Carlo with delight, jumping on his shoulders while he attempted to stay afloat.

"Be careful, Appoline! We're in the deep end!" He was holding on to her knees as she crawled on top of him, her silk shirt weighing heavily on her body.

"You speak English, too?" I called from my corner of the sea.

"Yes, I was told we'd be entertaining an American this evening."

Carlo was struggling to hold Appoline as she sang loudly across the bay. It wasn't until this exact moment that I realized the boom box sitting on the wooden marker next to the boys' discarded shoes (they had clearly prepared for this swim), was playing "Hearts and Bones." Paul Simon continued to sing to me all summer, whether through a stereo, the radios splattered across the market, my mom humming a tune, or Appoline shouting across the winds and waters. He was always singing.

"I appreciate the effort." I bellowed back to him.

"Of course! Are you ladies ready for our date tonight?" Carlo beamed at all of us.

"*Oui, mon bébé!*" Appoline soared above us all, coming to a stance on Carlo's shoulders, arms spread wide.

Her hair was plastered to her face, and I remember thinking quietly to myself that she didn't stay there long enough to give anyone an excuse to stare, but we all did because we were charmed, enthralled by her uncontrollable elegance.

François hollered at me from the dock and lifted me onto solid ground. We laughed as we slipped and shivered, the wind like melting ice on our backs. The four of us drowned the wharf with water and an explicable air of childhood mirth, running around in circles, attempting to dry off.

Up close, I could see why Appoline liked Carlo. He was handsome in a way that made sense when you pulled apart his features and looked at them individually. Dark, coarse hair flopped breezily atop his head and brushed over his eyebrows which were thick and masculine. His eyes were a deviating brown, and his jaw was straight edged. Yet, I happened to know that his hair fell like that because he was hiding a massive forehead and his eyes changed colors, not because of the sun, but because he was consistently losing interest in those around him.

Loosely, arms and legs flailing with eager anticipation, we jumped around the pier doing handstands and showing off our inability to complete a cartwheel without falling over.

"Come on, let's take this *date* back to my house." François winked at me.

"Why your house?" I asked.

"Because we're soaking wet, and last time I checked, you're a huge fan of my macarons."

"*Allez!*" Carlo yelled, pointing onward, upward and into the existing future, nearing just around the beaten path, closer to *now* than we had ever been or ever would be.

Frolicking in stride with the breeze, we arrived at François' house, skin damp and hands sweaty. His tiny abode sat in town, just around the corner from his bakery. The slatted roof and white brick looked clean and modest amongst the overgrown trees and wild bushes surrounding the exterior. If it weren't for the foliage, the hut would've been much more conspicuous from the main road. I realized in this moment that I had passed it numerous times before and never noticed the building just beyond the saplings.

"The cool thing about François," Carlo said jubilantly as we trekked up the gravel. "Is that he still lives with his mother."

François nodded his head, fake laughing with all the rest of us. Appoline pushed Carlo lightly and he turned to her, shrugging his shoulders.

"Be nice," she joked. "He's only forty."

"It's okay, I may live with my mother, but *Carlo's* mother happens to be a frequent house guest of mine," François retaliated.

"That's right, didn't you two go to school together?" Carlo bit back. We giggled and decided to ignore Carlo, for all our sakes.

Pulsating from the vibrancy of clotted laughter that resonated throughout our bodies like a passing virus, I saw the windows to the hut cracked open and laundry hanging down the sides. The linen wavered, embellishing the brick beneath. As we stepped inside and walked across the oak floors, I could imagine the socialites back east screaming at Appoline for her bare feet and unabashed enjoyment of small homes, cheap wine, and splintered ceilings.

No one spoke and no one objected as we stripped to our underwear, running around in the backyard, chasing any limb we saw, here or there, with the icy water from the garden hose. We took turns spraying one another down, measuring our efficiency of cleanliness by the seamless screams emerging from core to core. Frightened shrieks gusted the grass and hushed the tulips into hiding. At one point, François brought out a bar of soap, explaining it was more efficient this way.

I propped the backdoor open with a small stone when I heard Paul Simon singing from the radio on the granite kitchen countertop. I remember making a mental note: no baking supplies were in sight.

The couch next to the dining room table was worn and grumpy, a deep russet color, the kind that hid stains.

"Appoline! This is the song from the first night! At the pub!" I jumped and slid on the lawn, grabbing her hands, and twirling her.

"*Oui! J'adore ça! Danse avec moi!*" *Dance with me!* she squealed.

We took turns, spinning wildly, the boys joining in and skating on the wet grass, speeding off in a mess of directions. The radio announced that the song was named "Obvious Child." It called to the dotting of audience speckled across the country, even the ones who weren't listening. I smiled at Appoline and she nodded, certain of something I was unaware of.

Collapsed on the lawn, timid from our invading bodies, the four of us let the air above sink in, encompassing all of Earth on our sticky faces. One by one, we went inside to steal clothes from François' closet, which just so happened to be flooded with collared shirts exactly like the one I had given him.

Figuring I was making a statement by wearing one of the white and blue striped collared shirts, I pranced delicately into the living room after rinsing my feet, where everyone else sat comfortably, awaiting my arrival.

"We did it, four for four!" Appoline declared.

She jumped up from her bend in the couch and kissed me on the cheek, looping me around with giddy laughter. My eyes wavered, yet I noticed Appoline, François, and Carlo all had on collared shirts as well. We looked like a group of brokers who came home from a late night, remembering to unbutton their shirts, but forgetting to take them off. When realization crossed my face, everyone burst into riotous laughter.

"Was there a sale going on, François?" I joked, pinching his cheek and sitting precariously on his lap. "Are they multipurpose? Do you wear these shirts to bed, too?"

"No, I like to sleep naked." He said unbothered, staring me levelly in the eyes.

I caught myself by surprise, our bare legs overlapping. He didn't flinch, but I could feel his muscles tense as I leaned back into him, committing to the risk. This was the most intimate we had been, and blatantly so, embracing despite the lack of privacy. Appoline looked at me for a brief second, off guard. She quickly turned to herself, rummaging around the kitchen in an unnecessary fervor.

The only one who didn't seem to notice that the conversation had slipped and that I was choking on my actions, was Carlo. He was sprawled out on the other end of the couch, lounging with luster, and crooning in a deep, musty tone.

"Let's make dinner! François? Bake us something!" Appoline called from the kitchen.

Cabinets were clanging, but it was apparent this was for effect. She had no intention of cooking for anyone.

"I bake all day, all night, Appoline. Can a man ever get any peace?" François hummed lightly to her.

"I thought that's what your mother was for. Doesn't she cook for you?" Appoline murmured.

"No, our personal chef cooks for us. And our maid cleans, and my butler normally answers the door. I'm so sorry he wasn't here today; please forgive my rudeness. I'm sure you know all about *that,* Appoline." François was getting antsy.

I threw my arms around his neck, tracing his jaw with my fingers as he spoke. He hadn't shaved for a few days and the stubble on his chin tickled my knuckles. Behind him, I copied his head movements as he spoke with Appoline. She hid a smile.

"I'll cook." I said, popping up from François' lap and bouncing to join Appoline in the kitchen, curating a list in my head of all the dishes I knew how to make. I could have sworn, just for a moment, that François reached out instinctually, grasping at the air where I had just been.

"Well, in that case, I'll help," Appoline decided.

She looked delighted, as she found a bottle of red wine, a result from prying sneakily in the cupboards, and took a generous swig.

That summer, she accessorized with wine bottles. While her mom chased her around their marble castle with Hermès scarves and her dad sent money from his extended stays abroad, Appoline ran as quickly as she could, wine in hand, always searching for her next fix of cherry blood.

In this way, she was much like her mother, afraid she'd be unable to secure what she so desperately craved. Watching her gulp down the plum wine with satisfaction and an airy disposition, then discarding it nonchalantly to me, I realized she was lying to us all. Her calm demeanor steadied as she drank more and more, and she gloried in sharing this feeling, as if to say, *I'm only drinking this because it's here, right now, in the moment, not because I was seeking it all along.*

Chapter Ten

MY DEMISE BEGAN WHEN I found the frozen pizza hiding beneath the petrified fruits that littered François' freezer. Appoline and I had been sitting on the kitchen floor for twenty minutes, debating what to cook, weighing our skills and rating our ability to make something edible.

The boys had left us to fetch a few bottles of wine from Saul's, as Appoline had requested Beaujolais for the night's festivities. I was beginning to get warm from the wine settling on my tongue and decided to stick my head in the freezer, wherein I came face to face with our saving grace, better known as a Margherita pizza.

Dancing in celebration of our quick fix, we shoved the pizza in the oven and crawled on the countertop, sitting cross-legged across from each other. The warm breeze swirled in from the back door that was kept ajar, our summer night as warm as a hug.

"So, are you going to sleep with François tonight?" Appoline asked, sipping from the remains of the wine.

"I knew you had a hidden agenda when you sent them off to get more drinks." I laughed, standing up on the counter, pointing at her.

"I mean, I do want *Beaujolais*, but yeah I also wanted to gossip," she said, finding a loaf of bread near the cutlery and tearing off a piece.

Though she sat elegantly in front of a row of wine bottles filled to the brim, she'd still insisted that these weren't good enough. Tossing me the piece of crust, I caught it in my mouth as I stood above her.

"Damn," I said. "First try! I never get anything on the first try."

"Here," Appoline chewed thoughtfully on her own piece of baguette. "Try it again."

I prepped myself, bending my knees and opening my mouth, getting ready to make it two for two.

"One...two...three!" Appoline counted, throwing five different pieces of bread directly at my face. Leaning forward in an attempt to catch at least one, I fell. My hands broke my fall, straddling Appoline.

"*Oh là là.*" She laughed hysterically. I rolled over on the generous counter space and opened my mouth, showing her that I was slightly successful, as a piece of bread lay soggy on my tongue.

"Don't test my competitiveness, Appoline, I *will* win." My heart was thumping gallantly underneath François' collared shirt.

"If we play any games tonight, I want you on my team," she said, enthralled and impressed with my commitment.

"But do I want you on mine?" I teased, reaching past her to rip off another piece of bread.

"Ay! You're not even going to be hungry for the pizza!" she scolded me.

"Oh, my dear, you haven't seen me drunk eat. I am a bottomless pit. I am a monster who cannot be satiated. Try me," I said, mouth full and crumbs coating my lips.

"You are the master of avoiding questions, you know that?" Appoline smiled and raised her eyebrows.

I sat, pulling her up with me.

"I've probably learned that trade from you." I poked at her.

She gaped, mockingly offended. "Me? What? What could you possibly be talking about?"

"Everything! You've yet to tell me anything about what's been going on in your life, what your plans are. Every single day we talk about the moments directly in front of us, never the could be's, or what if's, or maybe's."

"Why would we talk about things that are uncertain, when there's so many absolute truths to enjoy?" she asked. I crossed my arms, pouting. Leaning closely to my face, she grabbed my chin. "What do you want to know, Belly?"

We both paused, laughing at her lapse in articulation.

"Belly! That's a new one," I said, nodding and finishing the entirety of the wine.

I tipped it upside down, questioning its legitimacy. "Can you—can you look and see?"

I ushered Appoline to put her face underneath the head of the bottle, shaking it as she did, droplets of red wine splattering her face.

"*Bah, merde!*"

She pushed me playfully, keeping her eyes closed as though the liquid would sting. Impulsively, I licked her cheek, slurping the wine from her face. Surprised, she opened her eyes quickly and I pulled away.

We stared at one another before laughing. Nothing felt strange, yet it was all layered in varying levels of risk. I knew I could gamble with her, taking my thoughtless and irresponsible chances.

"University," I said, my eyes glazing over from the alcohol.

"Right, university," she said, matter of fact. "I didn't go. Next."

"Why not?" I asked.

"Because I have a lot of money and not a lot of drive. Next," she reiterated.

"So then, what are your plans?" I continued on.

"Learn the family business, take over the hotel. Maybe I'll help open another one in Paris. That's been on my parents' radar lately. Next."

She was waving her hand, as if she had absolutely no time to indulge me in my mindless questions.

"Do you plan on staying in Saint __ de Vie for the rest of your life?"

My confidence grew with each passing moment, chasing my drunkenness, attempting to keep up.

"I run around all the time because I don't know what else to do, but I can't leave. I'm an only child. It's vital I do the one thing I can to make my parents happy. I'm the *heiress*." She said this last word with disdain and projection, as if propelling it out of her mouth, disgusted it even found its way in there.

"Next?" I asked.

"No," she said easily, not upset, but no longer compliant. "I have nothing left to say."

"You should come visit me in the fall," I offered.

"Where?" She tipped her head back, rolling the empty wine bottle between her hands.

"New York. I got a job working for a magazine editor," I said, bidding a soft smile. "I start a week after I return home."

"And how'd you snag that?" Appoline cocked her head sideways.

"One of my professors helped me. It was through an alumni program."

"I'm not surprised." She grinned flawlessly. "I would expect nothing less of you. Congrats, Belly. I've been wondering what you had to look forward to once you left us here."

"So...do you have any tips for me?" I asked bashfully, staring down into my lap.

"Tips?" Quizzically, she stood, stretching her arms and legs.

"Yeah...you know. For, if I do end up sleeping with him." My voice was a slight whisper now, and I kicked myself for being so embarrassed. This was Appoline. Sex was nothing more than an amorous interaction of drunken lust; a result of ardent limits, which were never to be regretted.

"Hm," Appoline was stumped.

"I—I've never been with an older man," I said, feeling the need to clarify.

"Ah." This seemed to make more sense to her. "But he's been with plenty of younger women. Don't let him fall for you. Your biggest risk is that he falls for you and you can never get rid of him. Older guys are like that. They find something young and beautiful and want to keep it forever, for themselves. Next thing you know, you're forty, taking care of a geriatric who can't even wipe his own ass. Your best years, gone. Selfish bastards." She chuckled knowingly to herself.

"Appoline...? Are you...jealous?" I laughed heartily, making fun of her passion.

"Hey, Belly, you asked for advice. I'm giving you some. Don't let that man have feelings for you. If you sleep together, leave before he wakes up. That's all I'm saying. If you don't, and tomorrow he introduces you to his mom as his fiancée, don't say I didn't warn you." She was cocky and walked around the kitchen, knowing so.

"SHIT!" I screamed.

"Quoi? Quoi!" What? What? Appoline jumped, afraid I was either offended or having a heart attack.

"The pizza!" I yelled, sprinting and jumping over her to wrench open the smoking oven.

//

Anchored to our embroidered chairs, Appoline, François, Carlo, and I peered uneasily at one another. I desperately begged myself not to laugh as both boys tried our pizza, brave eyes and warm smiles nodding at us. Appoline kicked me under the table, chugging a glass of Beaujolais in an attempt to hide her amusement.

The Margherita pizza was a beautiful shade of coal, rounded at the burnt edges, peaks of struggling mozzarella poking through. François took a bite, murmuring his adoration for our creation. Carlo looked at François incredulously, swallowing a rather large and unnecessary mouthful. I winced. He threw the pizza down on his plate.

"Well, girls," Carlo said, folding his hands on the table in front of him. "That is by far the worst pizza I've ever had, in my entire life. Absolutely the worst, congratulations. You've managed to ruin the one food I thought impossible to ruin..."

He turned to look at François, who was silently asking him with his eyes to cool it down.

"And I don't know who *you're* trying to lie to, you're a baker, this must be sacrilege to you."

The four of us sat there, holding in our breath, until Appoline spit her wine across the table, allowing madness to ensue. Tears ran down our faces as we laughed, miraculously at ease with Carlo's disconcerting honesty and François' feeble stab at trying to make us feel better.

"Your face!" Appoline was choking on her tongue.

"You looked so pained, François!" I said, laughing out my words in a throaty endeavor.

François shook his head and bent down, pulling out a steaming quiche from the bag by his feet.

"Good thing, I came prepared," he said, winking at Carlo.

"*Ah, bon.* Amazing!" Appoline raised her glass to him.

"*Merci beaucoup!*" I cheered in my worst French.

François set the quiche in the middle. Appoline and I, drunk from our first bottle of wine, reached gluttonously forward.

"Oh, no!" Carlo slapped our hands away, picking up the entire quiche and setting it on the plate before him.

"This is for us. You girls eat the divine pizza you made!" he joked, not allowing a smile to cross his face for fear of ruining his act.

"Come on now, Carlo." Appoline whined. She jumped up and sprawled across his lap, whispering sweetly in his ear. Her purring in French sounded like rain tapping a wooden ceiling, sensuously trying to sneak its way through the cracks. Almost immediately, he surrendered, placing the quiche back in the center. Doubled over in amusement, we demolished the quiche, rich with the carefree air of skinned grapes and adoration for backup plans.

"Cheers," I said, focusing on not slurring my words. "To Carlo and François' lack of trust in us!"

We all clanged glasses, murmuring in agreement.

//

"There's one piece left, who wants it?" Carlo eyed the table slowly, holding out the plate enticingly.

"I do!" I shot my hand at the quiche quickly.

Appoline and I exchanged looks as I winked at her, holding up the slice to my mouth.

"I will never get over your appetite," François commented, pulling my neck in the opposite direction to face his observations head on.

"I never run out of room." I shrugged after a moment, swallowing a bite of flavors only found in coastal markets of rounded women and wrinkled fishermen.

"Does that mean you're never content?" Appoline asked.

"No, it means she's never full," Carlo said, tapping his head, joking. "You must learn to eat slower, that's what my grandmother always told me. It helps."

I laughed, fully aware that some of us were analyzing my eating habits and others were analyzing my mind.

"It means I'm always hungry," I said, forcing the last bite dramatically in my mouth.

"Now, this is a good segue," Carlo pointed out, blissfully amused. "Let's do first impressions. Because I have to say, I didn't realize you were such an avid eater. When I first met you, I thought, okay, here's a girl who eats a normal amount. Now, I know you eat like a lion, you can't cook for shit, *and* you're much more exuberant when you've had a few." He motioned his hand to his mouth, as if drinking from an imaginary glass. We all laughed.

"Really? Okay. Well, when I first met you, I thought you were an immature little boy who had nothing better to do than swim in the harbor, as long as you were able to fix your hair afterward." My words were falling from my mouth.

"And?" Carlo tapped his fingers impatiently. "What's your verdict?"

"And now that I know you, I know I was right!" I joked, laughing with the table.

"Okay, no, no more. We're done playing this game." Carlo shook his head shyly, unconsciously running his fingers through his hair.

"Aha!" Appoline shouted, pointing at him.

In return, Carlo threw his hands up in concession, mumbling something about taking games too seriously.

After the dishes had been cleaned and put away, at François' insistence, the four of us spread out on the couch, bloated from wine and quiche and laughter.

"What time does your mom come home from the bakery today?" I asked.

"Oh, she's probably been home for a while now. We close at eight."

François had his head propped up on the corner of the couch, peering thoughtfully at me. Frantically, I looked around, concerned I was thrown into a Norman Bates situation and François' mom was sitting in the kitchen, solid and stuffed. François snorted, putting his arms around my shoulders.

"Calm down, she lives in the guest house, out back. Didn't you see it earlier?" he asked.

"I thought that was just a really fancy shed." I mumbled, my under eyes pink and warm.

Carlo and Appoline were whispering to one another on the cushioned lounge chair by the cobbled fireplace. Glancing over, I saw them entranced in lullabies and small kisses and greedy caresses. François pulled me close, focusing my thoughts on his coffee eyes, delicate enough to draw me in.

"Back to the game," he crooned.

"The game? François, I thought I had already proved that I can out eat you." I rolled my eyes.

"What was your first impression of me?" he asked, confident in an expectant and admiring answer.

Playfully, I walked my fingers from his jaw, down his neck, to the open ends of his matching collared shirt. He really was a beautiful man, and maybe, I thought, if I got close enough to him, his beauty would rub off on me.

"What was your first impression of *me*?" I countered.

"You mean before or after you threw up on me?" he asked, full of smooth-edged wit and twinkling eyes.

"You know what? I'm with Carlo on this one. Never mind, I don't want to play this game." I could feel my face getting red, so I looked down, my head now resting peacefully in the crook of his arm.

"I think I know what you thought of me." François said, parking his chin on the top of my scalp.

"*I* don't even know what I thought of you."

"Liar. You didn't like me. I could see it in the way you stood around me. On guard, rigid." François voiced his thoughts levelly.

I couldn't tell if he was amused or offended, and it concerned me that I was unable to make this discernment. Had he always been so hard to read, or was I simply too caught up in my own account of the season's events that I didn't bother to pay his advances any mind? I was beginning to question whether he actually fancied me, or if I was creating a fictional version of romanticized zeal and zest in the characters of my summer. I suddenly became very aware of my body on his.

"You're right. I didn't," I said evenly, deciding to leave my sprinkled dreams of creamy colors and felted caresses to drift without me for one evening.

In this moment, I wanted nothing more than translucent conversation and clear kisses.

"Well, I liked you right away," François said coolly, his jaw massaging my brow.

Sleepily, I murmured something to the effect of, "Why would you like me?"

"Because you're bright. I've never seen someone so unaffected by another's presence. It's like you could do with or without someone, and either way, you'd be okay. Your indifference, or maybe it's your independence, makes me want you to want me... Plus, I've never been with an American girl." François added this last bit, almost shamefully.

Meekly, I turned and looked him in the eyes.

"I'm American, but I'm also half French." I couldn't help but smirk. Red wine had always been a facilitator throughout my brief experience with drinking, but this Beaujolais appeared to be my downfall. I blamed Appoline for that.

Heartily laughing and picking up my wilting body, which was bogged down by plum wine and rich quiche, François scooped me into his arms and whisked me away to his bedroom.

Chapter Eleven

THE MUSIC THAT HAD carried us through the night halted when we tumbled deliciously into François' bed, soundless from the soft sheets and foamy mattress. Paul Simon's repetitive singing slowly faded, and all I could hear were the shutters tapping briskly, the seaside breeze blowing inland for a dance.

"Kiss me," I said lightly to François, overcome with the romance in his smile and the lust in his chest.

I said what he wanted to hear, and he drew me in, brushing my cheeks with his thumb. When he kissed me, it wasn't gentle or tender. He married his lips to mine, pressing deeply down into my soul, showing me what he had been longing for, what he had been wanting to do from the moment he first saw me.

Passionately, he sprung his body on mine, pulling my hair so my tongue had nowhere to go except mingle with his. Opening my eyes wide, I peered through the purple darkness to see François' eyes shut tensely, focusing adamantly and solely on my presence. I hated the way he looked, concentrating on my autonomy. Now I understood why lovers were always painted with their eyes closed in bed.

In a beat, he had pulled his collared shirt off my body, throwing it dramatically across the room. I swarmed beneath the heat of his breath, very aware that the only thing between me and immodesty was the blue cotton thong draped delicately around my hips. François moved his lips down my neck and his hands down my waist in succession, a melodious machine, well oiled.

I took a deep breath as I felt his forefinger lace in between my skin and cotton underwear, twisting in the mesh. François stopped and pushed himself up, so his chest was no longer grazing mine. I felt more vulnerable now than I had when he was skimming my panty line. Looking down into me, a space for hesitation between us, François spoke lightly.

"You're glowing." He ate eagerly with his eyes, tracing his right knuckle down my sternum, in between my breasts, circling my belly button, pausing before teasing the trembling in between my legs.

"That's because my summer tan hasn't stained my skin yet." I said briskly, slipping under his arm and out from underneath his broad shoulders, no longer waiting for whatever was to come next.

He surrendered to my light nudge, as if my prey, and collapsed on his back. He was handsome lying there, peering at me, amused and entranced.

"You're not used to women being coy, are you, *Monsieur Fortin?*" I couldn't help but lick my lips as I spoke again, thoroughly exulting in my dominance.

At this, François pulled me down, strong and greedy, with his hands on the rounds of my butt, even paler than the rest of me.

"*Monsieur Fortin?* I like it when you call me that, makes me feel like a man." François said, pushing himself into me.

"Oh, the half-naked woman on top of you wasn't enough to make you feel like a man?" I countered.

"You know, you don't talk a lot, but when you do, it's always repartee." François was tasting my neck as he whispered his concerns to that half-naked woman lying on top of him.

"I just don't know peace." Joking, I rolled over and threw the sheets over my head.

"What are you doing?" François poked his fingers at me through the fabric. Gently, he lifted the sheet, and joined me in the dark, lying stiffly shoulder to shoulder.

I hesitated to respond.

"Are you tired?" he asked.

"Not necessarily, but the Beaujolais has me feeling all tingly."

"Are you sure it's not me that has you feeling that way?" François tilted his head in the crevice of my neck, angled away from him.

"Could be a dangerous combination of both," I said simply.

François sighed, and I began to grow anxious, as I could tell his impatience was heightening. In truth, my heart was slamming in my chest. I was afraid if François touched me, my skin would electrocute him. Why was this man, this grown man with a business and a life and women at his feet, in bed with me?

"Hey, let's go chug the rest of the bottle," I said enticingly, sitting up and covering my chest with the sheets. I pouted at him, letting my bottom lip dangle.

"Of the Beaujolais?" he asked, raising his eyebrows.

"*Oui.*" I jumped up, searching aimlessly for his discarded shirt.

"But we've already finished off two."

"Then what's one more?" I asked, demure, alluring François with my soft eyelashes and bare breasts, covered only by his fancy collared shirt.

"I'll race you," I sang.

At this, François jumped from the bed and ran to the kitchen. Laughing, I trailed behind him, shutting the door quietly yet firmly after me.

After tiptoeing sneakily on the slippery wooden floors and ransacking the cabinets for wine glasses, François and I stood aloof in the middle of the kitchen, goblets full of liquored grape juice. I counted to three, specifically in French to impress the host, and then the both of us tipped back the wine and chugged, racing to see who would finish first.

It was difficult to come to an agreement about who the champion was, but once I began unbuttoning my shirt, François gave in and surrendered to my obvious victory. Bowing down, he raised his arms to me. Twirling, I accepted his defeat and laughed loudly. To our surprise, we heard a cough from the couch.

"Shit. Shh," I whispered.

"I forgot they were here," François mumbled.

He grabbed my hand to usher me back to his bedroom, but not before I had the chance to squint and see Appoline lying alone on the couch, devoured by the oversized pillows. Carlo's body hadn't even left an imprint.

//

Morning came, as it always does, with a swell of wind and salt arising from the garrulous sea. Upon opening my eyes, I realized two things: one, being that I was extremely hungover, and two, being that I had no idea where I was. Thankfully, the window was propped open and I could see the ocean's waters swaying intimately in the backyard.

The roaring stream of turrets building and crashing in the sea assured me I was safe. As long as I could see the marina, I knew I was going to be all right.

As if time could hear my thoughts, François walked in the bedroom just seconds after I gathered my bearings, smiling gleefully and humming "Obvious Child." It sounded out of key coming from his mouth. I winced.

"Good morning, Bellamy." He kissed me on the forehead as I lay frozen, newly aware that I was shirtless. François continued down my collar bone, kissing me lightly. Quickly, I stopped him.

"François...last night...we didn't..." My voice trailed off as I remembered our wine chugging contest and the mess of kisses that proceeded it.

"Non." He shook his head slightly, sighing. "No, after all that Beaujolais, we just went to sleep. Don't you remember?"

A wash of relief filled my chest, cleansing my pores. I didn't mind if he wanted to keep kissing me now.

"Yeah, actually I do. We both felt too good to let anything ruin that moment, that feeling. We were content," I said, more to myself than to him.

"Well, I mean, you fell asleep, but sure. Anyway, I made you and Appoline breakfast. Come."

François tossed me my clothes from the day before, wind-dried and stale, then walked out to give me privacy.

I sat in his bed for a moment, somewhat offended that he hadn't offered me his shirt, and wondering if it had anything to do with the fact that I hadn't offered him *myself* the night before. Pushing these thoughts quickly out of my head, I dressed and joined François and a heavy-eyed Appoline at the kitchen table.

Just as I was preparing to dive into a deliciously warm meal, Appoline jumped up from her seat, explaining that she had to rush back to the hotel to meet her mom for breakfast. Out of instinct, I insisted on walking back with her, as I wanted to shower and stretch my legs. We both kissed François goodbye, thanked him for his hospitality, and capered carelessly past the front door, into the fresh day unsoiled by our footsteps for only a few seconds longer.

François waved sullenly from the entry, disappointed we didn't take any croissants with us. I had told him to share with his mother, as I was sure she would appreciate the surprise. Crossing the cobblestone path that led to the main street, I caught up to Appoline, who was meandering, having lost her incessant haste.

"Hey. So, how was last night? Where did Carlo go?" I asked, clawing at the trail of hair shimmering down her back.

"He left," she said, reaching up and grabbing a handful of cherries from the tree that forged a stride of shade above us.

"What? Why? When?"

"Because, Bellamy, that's how you keep things clean. No mess. I told you this...and I don't know. Probably this morning."

She viciously tore into the cherries in her palm, juice dribbling down her chin. Appoline was a beautiful mess of savagery, violently overbearing as she crippled the cherry pits, squeezing them between her fingers. I didn't bother to tell her I knew Carlo had left before the sun was up. He had left her in the night, to sleep unaware and alone. There was no need to tread on her clearly annoyed and clearly very bruised ego.

"Did you guys have sex?" I asked, pretending to be caught up in shading my eyes from the sun.

Alas, in truth, I just didn't want her to look at me with her rounds of twinkling irises. It would have been too much to hear her answer while bearing her heavy gaze at the same time.

"We do every night we spend together," was her quick reply.

I nodded slowly, stopping in my tracks as she continued to walk. Wiping the excess of splattered cherry juice from her face, she turned back, exasperated that I hadn't kept up with her.

Standing on the tips of my toes, I jumped, ripping cherries from the tree limb overhead. Appoline put her hands on her hips, acknowledging the standoff we had found ourselves in. Rolling the fruit from hand to hand, I cocked my arm and threw a cherry over to Appoline, who bent her knees and tilted her head back just in time to catch it gracefully in her mouth, swallowing it whole.

"How did the pit taste?" I called to her.

"As good as any pit would," she finally giggled, and I felt my fingers regain movement.

I hadn't realized I had been holding air hostage from my lungs until I coughed up cherry skin, a crude reminder that blood was the same color.

Appoline and I walked perilously along the edge of the marina after we passed through town. I was waiting patiently for her to continue speaking. From the way she held her arms tightly to her side and opened her mouth in syncopation with her steps, the pretense was all but unavoidable.

"Well, I had fun last night. Carlo is... a lot," I finally offered, paving an avenue for her thoughts to glide down.

"We *do* every night we're together," Appoline repeated abruptly, not in response to my contribution to the conversation. "But we didn't last night."

Feeding off her hesitancy, the pair of us ambled leisurely up the rounded cliffs, the shore only a sandy stretch of beach away. Clouded from fog, the windows to my grandfather's cottage were the only crisp outline I could see peering up above.

"You didn't," I repeated.

"Nope." Bashfully, she kept her head down, shuffling the heels of her feet.

"He left last night, Appoline. He didn't wait until morning." I threw up these words, wishing I had just swallowed them in disgust instead.

"I know." She grabbed a few stones that sat cratered in between the sidewalk and the dunes. Pocketing them, she patted her shirt, making sure they were secure against her breast.

"We had a fight. I told him I didn't want to sleep with him because we were on François' couch, and you were both in the other room. I just didn't... I don't know. Anyway, he left."

Her face had changed, and her strained shrug camouflaged the sorrow that she wore, the innocence of her cheeks shining through.

"Anyway," she went on, a bit more forcefully now. "He left. But you stayed. And I warned you about staying. You stayed, Bellamy, and now you're going to get pulled in. I told you not to stay until the morning when you sleep with someone. And look what you did! You've probably ruined our whole summer now. We're not going to be able to enjoy anything, because you're going to be wrapped up in François, fighting, then having sex, then fighting some more! All of this could've been avoided, if you had just listened to me and left before he woke up, but you didn't. You stayed."

Appoline was heaving, her chest concaving, and her forehead furrowed in a stream of senseless anger.

"Appoline, my dear," I said, trying very desperately not to laugh in her face. "You never gave me any rules about staying until the morning after when you *don't* sleep with someone."

Cheekily, I pinched her nose and leapt a few paces ahead of her. Flustered, Appoline ran to my side, spinning me around with a pull of my hand.

"What do you mean you didn't sleep with him? You spent the night in his bed. You drank a lot of Beaujolais, and I mean a lot. He wants you. You said you liked him, too."

She couldn't seem to fit the pieces of our drunken night together. When sex wasn't involved, the puzzle couldn't be completed.

"I don't know. I didn't want to. We drank and then fell asleep. Who cares? It doesn't even matter." I shrugged.

"It does though. Did he get upset? Do you think he's going to take you out again? Are you a *tease*, Bellamy?"

She attempted to mock me with this last question, but I could hear the urgency and persistence in her voice.

"No, he didn't get upset. He's a man. He can handle rejection. Maybe he likes me enough to wait for me."

As I said this, I quickly reached my hand down Appoline's front pocket, searching for the stones she had stowed away.

"Hey!" she yelled, swatting at my hand to remove it.

I didn't relent, squeezing harder to grab hold of the stones.

"Why did you put those in here?" I asked, aggressively demanding an answer. Constantly flexing my hand inside her shirt pocket, I fumbled around, trying to gather all the stones. As Appoline tightened her grip on my wrist, she pulled futilely to remove my hand, but instead, I accidentally grabbed her breast.

I let the stones fall from my palm inside her pocket, so I could fully caress her breast. Stalemate. We stood there, on the coastal sidewalk, caught between a bustling town and a sleepy village of cottages and grandparents. Our chaotic disarray of pirouetting words and jarring opinions gathered between my lips and hers.

I held her for a moment longer, allowing her heart to beat under the shield of my hand, protecting it from the carnage and violence that encapsulated the very worst of this world. Grazing her breast with the most sensitive part of my palm, I felt her nipple through her shirt, hard and perky. Appoline's eyes fluttered, as if she were waking up after a very long sleep. Maybe I was waking up, too.

"Let go of me," she said, no longer pulling at my hand, but waiting patiently for me to release my grip.

In one slick movement, I slipped my hand from her breast and searched quickly for the stones, grabbing them, and pulling them out to gloat in her face.

"Aha! What are you doing with these? When did you become a stone collector?" I asked, spinning with delight.

Crossing her arms across her chest, she said, "I was trying to weigh myself down. Scared I was going to fly away in this wind, one day."

"You're adorable when you're upset," I said, laughing freely.

"He doesn't like you enough to wait for you," Appoline pointed out. "He just wasn't ready to pressure you into it. He has to ease himself into your trust."

"What?" This statement caught me off guard.

She sounded as though she was coming from a place of bitterness and resentment. "François. He's not going to wait for you. No one likes anyone enough to do that."

"Maybe I'm different," I said.

"You're not, Bellamy. No one is. He's a thirty-six-year-old man who could get any girl in town. He's not going to beg to have you." Her eyes pitied me.

"You said Carlo was a nice guy, but he left last night because you wouldn't sleep with him," I shot back.

"And François will leave you too, Bellamy, whether it's after you give him what he wants or before you ever do."

"Yesterday, you said he'd fall for me if I slept with him." I grimaced as my voice cracked.

"Well, today, I'm telling you he'll leave you. He'll suck you dry and steal your youth. All he wants you for is the prize in between your legs." Appoline was red in the face, fists clenched by her side. "Why do you think a man who's almost forty is hanging out with a bunch of people in their twenties? Because he wants to fuck you! That's it!"

"Maybe that's how guys are with you because you go around sleeping with the whole town, but that's not how anyone looks at me. I have worth and I know it. That's the difference between you and me."

"You have no right to stand there and judge me. All I've done is try and be your friend, show you a good summer, and trust you with my secrets." She was shouting now.

"Secrets? It's no secret you sleep with any villager who shows even the slightest bit of interest in you at all, Appoline! You haven't trusted me with anything. You're just jealous François actually likes me and the best *you* can find is a late night who doesn't stick around for you in the morning. You don't want me to have François because then you wouldn't have anyone to hang out with. You want me all to yourself, but you won't even be honest about it."

Regret seeped into my eyes as soon as I yelled these words at her. Appoline took a step back from me, even though she was already a yard away. She stared directly into my eyes, her own welling up with crystal tears that were so delicate they almost looked like jewels.

"Say something!" I screamed. Angrily, I threw the stones at the ground in front of us. One cracked. I heard her sigh from the expanse before me.

"Those stones were for your grandfather, since he's always looking for new ones."

Her voice didn't falter as she adjusted her shirt, turned around, and walked away from me. She paced down to the dock, past the floating gaggle of boats and fishermen, all too concerned with their bait to notice that the drizzle of mist in the air had become a torrential rainfall.

//

I spent an hour sitting on the floor of my bedroom, attempting to glue the cracked stone back together. Guilt and shame felt like weights residing on my chest, lowering me to the ground.

Refusing to sit comfortably on my bed until I repaired my rash mistake, I tumbled inside my mind, not only upset that I had been so harsh to Appoline, but also worried I had offended her by touching her breast. Embarrassment rolled over the hunches of my back, as I realized she had probably lashed out at me because she was uncomfortable that I had touched her in such an intimate way.

Enraged with my own idiotic actions, I chucked another full, brightly spotted stone, at the wall across from me. This one also cracked, and I let out a scream that probably could have cracked the stone itself. I sat there, on the floor, secluded and surrounded by two stones, now broken into four haphazard pieces.

"Bellamy? Why are you breaking stones inside your grandfather's house?" My mom had rapped lightly on my bedroom door before peeping her head around the corner.

"It's self-expression," I mumbled sardonically.

"Well, can you express yourself outside next time? Look what you did to the wall." My mother sighed and walked across the room. "Where were you last night?" she asked gently, sensing flames of rage and frustration, but careful not to reignite the fire.

"It doesn't matter," I answered. "Can you just help me glue these back together?"

"Honey, you know I'm horrible with arts and crafts."

I rolled my eyes at her, amazed with her wit and ability to find humor even amidst my obvious mental breakdown.

"I knew I should've taken Home Economics in high school," I faintly muttered.

"Listen, darling. Why don't you go out on the boat today with Papaly? He wants to take you rowing on the canoe. Could be a nice time to spend with him." Cross-legged in front of me on the floor, she was limber and elegant at fifty.

"Maman, the rocks," I whined.

"You need to go to sea, sit in the middle of nothing, with no escape, and just breathe, *mon bébé*. You can throw as many rocks as you want out there. They won't hit anything and they won't snap when they break water, either."

Knees cracking as she stood, my mother leaned down and kissed me atop my head, gathering strands of my hair together before pulling it gently into a braid.

"You used to enjoy this when you were younger," she said.

"I used to enjoy a lot of things." I cradled all four broken pieces of the stones in my hands.

"This afternoon, okay? You and Papaly. Canoe."

"It was raining earlier," I pointed out.

"Does it make a difference if the water is above or below you? You're on a boat either way."

At this final statement, my mom swept away peacefully from my room, leaving me to dwell in the suffocation of self-pity and dwindling anger.

Chapter Twelve

MIRACULOUSLY, THE SKY FLAUNTED its infinite power and decided to transition into the afternoon with bright clouds and dry eyes. The wind whipped against my grandfather's face, chapping his cheeks. I wish the wind knew how to kiss, instead.

Rowing through the streams of seaweed and granules of sand that congealed at shore, we pushed off into the vast and sultry waters, waters that had known many men and women before us.

Papaly grunted and waved as fishermen with wrinkles carved into their hands called out to us. Once we found ourselves gently bobbing in a more secluded area of the cosmic stretch that sparkled magnificently against the grainy shore, Papaly clapped his hands together and began rummaging around in the wicker basket he'd brought with him.

I skimmed my hand atop the restless waves, wondering what chapter of my summer this morning's altercation would fall into. I certainly didn't want it to be the last.

Excitedly, Papaly handed me a plate and pulled out a baguette, still warm from the oven. I laughed, surprised. Seeing my amusement, he held up his finger, signing for me to wait a moment longer. Delving back into the wicker basket, he popped up, holding three different types of cheeses and a board of sliced ham. I cheered with delight as he stood and did a small twirl, tipping his imaginary hat at me.

In my best French, I asked him if we had anything to drink. I was immediately given a paper cup and a sly look. For his final surprise, Papaly pulled out a mini bottle of champagne and sang, "*Je te donne,*" as he watched me gulp down my first cup.

Giddy and boyish, Papaly leaned back in the canoe, chewing thoughtfully on his baguette and breathing in the daylight. Overhead, seagulls sang to one another. I counted three birds circling our floating abode before I remembered my pocket was heavy.

"Here, *tiens*," I said, handing Papaly one of the two previously broken stones. It was now glued together scrappily, but he had to have it. I knew it belonged to him.

"*Pour toi.*" *For you,* I told him. From Appoline and I.

Moments passed before his eyes turned glossy, closing his hand around the stone that lay perfectly in the center of his palm.

"*Pour elle.*" *For her,* he said.

His voice was small, but strong. Cocking my head sideways, I gave him a quizzical look. For whom?

Papaly dropped the stone in the breast pocket of his nautical vest, just as Appoline had earlier. After wiping his hands, he shifted sideways, scooting closer to me and revealing the wooden paneling at the tip of the canoe that he had been sitting in front of.

Centered at chest height, plastered to the water-stained bark, was a picture of my grandmother. I looked at Papaly, as if asking for permission, then leaned in, peering at the vibrant photo of Mamaly.

Surrounded by small bushes and colorful foliage, my grandmother stood brightly, pictured in front of their seaside cottage with the natural life around them, youthful and in growth. She was smiling, her arms held out, as she showed off a heap of stones cradled in her hands.

Squinting, I noticed there were just a few stones laid on either side of her, outlining the path to the doorway. My grandmother was beautiful, radiating life, the gems of the earth scattered among her vitality. Turning back to my grandfather, I smiled softly.

Papaly nodded, and I reached out to squeeze his hand. He had pulled out the stone from his pocket, and was holding it once again, cherishing her memory, warm against his skin.

"*Pour elle,*" I said, the wind and the waves catering melodiously to our afternoon at sea.

//

Resigned to the ache of melancholic hunger masticating within me, I ran into town late that evening and bought myself an ice cream before the shops closed. It hadn't occurred to me that I didn't need to wait for Appoline to enjoy a colorful frozen custard. Licking the cream melting deliciously down my arm, I imagined she was there with me, anyway.

Lucidly, I strolled through the streets, misty with salt and dampening from the night seeping in. Villagers bounded to and from, no particular destination in sight. It was a leisurely evening. La Baleine Bleue glowed with a generous tapering of light, so naturally, I decided to pop my head in, enjoying this time with myself.

Sitting at the bar with a cherry flavored ice cream cone in one hand and a gin and tonic in the other, I challenged myself to chug my drink before the custard had a chance to drip profusely over the already sticky counter. The barman smiled kindly and passed me a glass bowl from behind the bar, nodding toward my cone. Recognizing the inevitable had never been my strong suit, I blushed.

"*Merci.*" I swallowed as I held out my hand. "Oh, and uh, *s'il vous plaît ...*"

Before I could finish scrambling in my broken French, the barman gently placed another gin and tonic, prim and proper, in front of me.

"On my house," he said in a thick and throaty accent. "Your granfazzer found me a rare bottle of Château Margaux. Worth much more zan zis drink. Whatever you want, you can 'ave."

"*Oh, là là. Merci beaucoup,*" I said, eyes wide.

"He's a good man. Retired, but always trying to help zis town. He never comes down for a drink anymore, though. Let him know we miss 'im 'ere."

With a final swipe of his towel, the barman shook his head and walked away. Slightly stunned, I stared after him for a moment before raising my glass to the empty space in front of me and guzzling down round number two. Picking up my melted bowl of ice cream, I lifted it to my lips. Sipping greedily, I finished up the job.

"So, was your dinner good?" A man to my left swooped next to me, brushing my arm. Carlo appeared, laughing as he steadied my hand on the bowl that he almost made me drop.

"Ugh, Carlo," I said.

He smiled pleasantly, waiting for my answer.

"Why would you assume this is my dinner?" I asked, rolling my eyes.

"Because." He was eating up every second of this. "When someone doesn't have sex, they eat ice cream for dinner."

Proudly, he crossed his arms and looked at me, expecting this provocation to spark something in me.

"In that case, you should be eating some, too," I said lazily, unimpressed with his icebreaker.

"So, she told you we got into a fight, huh?" Carlo, acquiescent now, lumbered over and fell onto the stool next to me.

"Yeah. And *he* told you." I flagged down the barman for round number three. "Not that I thought there was anything really to tell," I added.

Carlo laughed. "I envy you, Bellamy." He turned to the barman. "*Louie, tiens.*" He paid him for both of our drinks.

"Louie..." I repeated under my breath.

"What?" Carlo was stuffing his wallet back into his pants.

"Nothing. Thanks for the drink."

"Of course, you're clearly having a rough night," he pointed out. "Cheers."

I didn't even bother contradicting him. That would've taken too much effort, and I was already feeling the burn from the gin becoming complacent in the back of my throat.

"Woah, calm down." Carlo pulled the drink away from my mouth just as I cleared the glass. "What's the point in getting blindingly drunk if you're not even going to make any bad decisions? Women."

"You've been saying a lot of precarious things, Carlo, but I refuse to give in. I won't do it," I said.

"Oh, come on. Why not? Indulge me." He was drinking neatly from his glass of Scotch.

"You envy me?" I looked at him dubiously.

"I do. I mean that."

I waved my hand at him to continue.

"You're naïve, but it's endearing."

"François likes me," I said, attempting to convince the both of us.

"Of course he does. As does Appoline. Hell, maybe I do, too." Setting his glass down, he sighed deeply. "And you're pretty and fun and witty enough to string someone along. Now, I'm not so sure how I feel about you being a virgin, but that's not the point. Eventually, whoever it may be, they're going to get tired of the chase. Your innocence and timidity are going to push them away."

He finished this longwinded monologue with a demand for another round of drinks.

Stupefied, I sat there staring straight ahead until Louie set two more glasses on the table, crystal ice cubes floating peacefully in their home of cool liquid. I snatched them both up before Carlo could object and downed the pair with unsettling ease. Opening his mouth to speak, I cut him off quickly, holding my finger up as a weapon.

"Listen to me, Carlo." I was fierce even though my eyes were having trouble focusing on his face now.

The air in the bar was brassy, yellow light growing beneath the lacquered ceiling. His eyes were dark and bold against the bruising ambience, blurred from the pallor of rain fogging the windows.

"I am not a virgin," I said.

"Then why are you whispering?" Carlo replied softly, ducking his head in closely to mine.

"I feel as though I was speaking rather loudly," I answered defiantly.

"Your cheeks are red."

"It's from your Scotch."

"Come on Bellamy, there's no use in lying to me. I know." He pressed his weathered hand against my face, stroking my chin amicably. Arrogance coupled with pity in the crevice on his chin.

"I thought you said you envied me." Apprehensively, I coughed and pushed him away.

Sighing, he ordered yet another glass, warning me this time. "This one is mine, okay?"

I clinked my two empty drinks, the one meant for me, and the one I'd stolen from Carlo, otherwise unresponsive.

"You already had those two. This one is mine; it's not for you to take." He sipped lightly on his Scotch, unrelenting and firm in his grasp.

Leaving money on the counter for Louie, I stood, gathering all parts of myself with an unbalanced effort.

"She's at the pier," Carlo called, his back turned toward me now. "I think she's waiting for you."

"Appoline never waits for anyone." I replied. "You should know that."

Gently, I patted him on the shoulder, trying to convey a sense of apology despite us both being aware that I had nothing to apologize for.

"Maybe she's not waiting for you, but you'll show up anyway." His back caved underneath my hand, his muscles sullen and overworked.

"Thanks for the drinks, Carlo. That one's on me." I nodded to Louie, who winked as I shuffled to the door through sleepy villagers.

With growing curiosity and a false confidence running through my veins, I faced the open bar of bent and groggy townies comparing brown ales in hushed, yet light conversation.

"DO I LOOK LIKE A VIRGIN?" I yelled to the room after clearing my throat, considering any reason at all to stop myself.

Gradually, as if time had decided to think in slow motion, each drinker and pool player and dart thrower alike stopped to raise their eyes at me. Confusion. Carlo hid a smile, finally getting the emotion he had tried so hard to evoke from me.

Concerned voices questioned me in French, unclear on what I had called out to the audience. Frozen, I forced myself to raise my arms and push a rigid smile on my face.

"I mean, *bisous et bonne nuit!" Kisses and good night!* I shouted apprehensively, the onlookers sipping dark liquor as they watched me teeter uncomfortably.

"*A votre santé!*" Carlo jumped in from his seat at the bar, raising his glass and insisting everyone else do the same.

When realization swept over the good French people of La Baleine Bleue that night, they all murmured loudly in agreement.

"*A votre santé!*" was their congenial response.

I implored Carlo a *thank you* with my eyes and rushed out of the pub, but not before shouting, "*Vive la France,*" as adrenaline and drunkenness had overcome me.

//

The rain embedded seamlessly into my hair, untidy and loose around my face. I hadn't worn it down all summer, but tonight I shook it out, tired of the knot pulling at the top of my head. By the time I turned down the avenue of docked boats and coiled ropes, the pier was slick from rainfall.

On the very edge of the wharf was Appoline, sitting upright, her feet dangling just slightly above the black water. She wasn't sleeping this time. Nervously, I approached, deciding humbly to sit down next to her.

"You're getting water on me," she said, not turning to look at me.

My feet swayed beside hers, but I made sure they didn't touch. "It's raining, Appoline, and you're sitting on a dock."

"Right, and you're getting even more water on me." She was insistent.

I had never despised the smell of sea salt and sodden wood more than I did in that moment.

"Listen," I began, chilly with anticipation. "I'm sorry for what I said. I was angry."

"Why were you angry?" she asked, stoking the fire.

"Because." I took a deep breath. "Because I felt as though you were implying my worth is only measured by my—by what's in between my legs...and who I let in."

My face was heating up. I stared into the sky, hoping God's tears would take away my humiliation.

Appoline sighed, handing over a bottle of red wine, still without looking at me. The only light came from the moon above. I took this as a peace offering and drank greedily from it. In true Appoline style, she pulled out another bottle, this one for herself. We drank in silence.

"I was jealous François would still be into you even though Carlo left the very *moment* I didn't give him what he wanted," she finally admitted, sipping generously from her contrasting bottle of white wine.

"Prosecco?" I asked, nodding at the bottle.

"Vodka," Appoline answered. "I find there's less judgment this way."

"Why does it matter if it's wine or vodka? It's all alcohol," I said.

"One is much stronger than the other, Bellamy."

"You don't have to be jealous," I wavered, my tongue bitter from the wine. Appoline took a deep swig of her vodka. From her shadow on the boardwalk, it looked like she pursed her lips as though they stung.

"I can't stay away from you," I added, even though it wasn't me she was worried about.

From my pocket, I pulled out the other stone that I had broken earlier that day. It was ugly, and it was obvious it had been broken in half, but it was glued together, nonetheless.

"Here." I set the stone on the dock beside her hand. "My peace offering. You and I."

I didn't wait to see if she'd pick it up. Instead, I rose and began to walk down the marina.

"Tomorrow," I called over her stooped shoulders. "Tomorrow, let's go to dinner. I haven't been out to eat yet. I'm craving coq au vin!"

"Come to the hotel at seven," she replied lightly.

I nodded to myself, walking away against the rain. Apologies had been made and dinner plans were set. All the while, I never even saw her face.

//

When I arrived home, my mother reprimanded me.

"What? You take strolls now in the pouring rain? You're going to get sick!" She ushered me inside, yanking a towel from the hall closet.

"You get even more wet if you run. So, I walked," I replied. "Plus, weren't you the one who was telling me earlier this morning that it didn't matter if the water was above or below me?"

"Ugh," my mother said as she waved her hand. "I was just trying to be encouraging. I wanted you to have a fun day with your grandfather...not catch pneumonia while you were at it."

"At what age does the scolding stop?" I rolled my eyes with a smile.

"Whatever age your common sense kicks in," she replied.

I laughed and crept toward her as she began to set a kettle on the stove.

"Oh, no. You stay away from me. Go change and put on warm clothes while I make you some tea," she scolded.

"Come on, hug your daughter," I smiled broadly, tantalizing her as I chased her around the kitchen.

Slipping, I left a trail of puddles behind me. My mom finally gave up running away from me and instead cautioned me to be careful of the stove before I tackled her to the tiled kitchen floor.

"Honey, shush. Papaly is sleeping." She tried to reign in the burst of energy that had erupted from me.

"It's nine," I said.

We sat now with our backs against the wooden cabinets, drinking warm tea and huddled beneath a congress of bath towels that smelled of fresh chamomile, pressed with lavender.

"He had a long day. Rowing out to sea in that canoe. It takes a lot out of an old man," my mom shared.

"Papaly's not an old man," I responded. "He's Papaly."

"He can still be Papaly, even though he's old."

"Hey, did you know he found an expensive bottle of wine for Louie at La Baleine Bleue?" I asked.

"You need a change of pace. You should not be spending every night out drinking at that bar." She shook her head.

"Mom, I hate to break it to you, but I get free drinks now, anytime I want." I was proud as I crossed my arms and sat back, the cabinet handle digging into my skin. "You can thank Papaly for that."

"I remember Louie," my mom said as she sipped her tea. "How's he doing?"

"Better now that Papaly found him that wine. He said he misses him. That Papaly never goes out for a drink anymore."

My mom was silent.

"Do you miss traveling and seeing the world?" I asked.

"Me?" She looked surprised, tapping her mug thoughtfully. "Sometimes. But eventually, I stopped caring about what I was seeing and started caring more about who I was seeing it with." Mother smiled and put her arm around my shoulders. "Coming here every summer with you was my favorite thing. I wouldn't trade it for all the wonders in the world," she said, pinching my chin.

"Maman, stop it," I whined, although secretly I basked in her adoration for me.

"You're my little eighth wonder," she added, squeezing my cheek. "I'm going to miss making you tea at night once you go back to New York."

"You might not realize this maman, but you're allowed to make me tea in New York, too."

"No? You don't say?" she said facetiously. "Well in that case, I might have to move in with you. How do you feel about splitting a two bedroom?"

"I swear, you've gotten funnier with old age." I laughed.

"And you've gotten meaner." She held me close, brushing the top of my scalp with her fingers.

"I'm going out to dinner tomorrow night," I mentioned lightly, letting my words tiptoe across to her ears.

"Oh, that'll be fun." She stood to pour more hot water into her mug, discarding her questions loosely. "With whom?" she asked.

"Appoline."

"François too? And, uh, that boy..." My mom was snapping her fingers, searching for a name.

"Carlo. His name is Carlo." I swallowed, much tenser than I needed to be. "No, they're not coming. It's a girl's night."

Spinning around from the stove, my mother, charmingly unaware, smiled softly.

"Well, that should be fun...maybe I can join?" she joked.

"When Amélie comes out too, we'll let you know." I laughed as I lumbered over to the sink and set my mug down.

"I still can't believe that woman is from Providence, Rhode Island and has a name more French than mine," my mom said, shaking her head.

"Clearly, her family has always had an affinity for France," I winked, rising to kiss her good night.

"Hey," my mom called as I turned to leave the kitchen. "Where are you going?"

"To put on warm clothes. Trying not to catch pneumonia, remember?" I teased.

Exhaustion hit the back of my neck and settled near the rounds of my eyes as I let the damp bath towels fall to the floor of my bedroom.

The day had been an extensive study of my character, and I could feel all the inner workings of my psyche being pitted against one another, in search for gratification. Truthfully, I was content in this moment. I didn't have a full grasp of peace, but I was content.

Too enamored with the Ferris wheel of enervated emotions running amok inside my head, I crawled atop the mound of towels that sat on my wooden floor. Tugging at my wet clothes, I sighed and fell promptly asleep, my soaked shirt pulled halfway over my head.

Chapter Thirteen

IN MY PAST LIFE, had I lived one, I know I was a carpenter. Crowded stickily in my compact bedroom, I jumped and pointed with excitement at the hummingbirds congregated just beyond my window. The morning was flooded with visions of fleeting colors, birds chirping harmoniously around the wooden birdhouse I had built when I was six. It hung from a spruce tree, sturdy and safe.

Squealing with glee, I begged my groggy mother and grandfather to revel in the glory of this jovial morning and the clean air that accompanied it. Judging from the tedious looks they shared behind my back, they were clearly worried I had forgotten about the simple pleasures of nature, earth, life.

"You're not understanding!" I whined. "It's an omen. A good one!"

Faint whispers of clipped music poked and prodded the expanse between my window and the birdhouse. I stretched my head through the bay window, pleading with the birds to never cease their singing.

"One would only find birds squawking a good omen if they were expecting a bad one." My mom brushed off my exclamation with her own sleepy judgment, only half believing what anyone had to say.

She sighed, using the mug in her hands to keep her warm. The mornings in Saint __ de Vie had been abnormally chilly that summer.

I turned to Papaly, heartfelt eyes seeking validation. "Papaly..."

"*Oui...oui! C'est magnifique!*" Papaly reassured me, kissing his fingers to his lips.

"This is why I like him more than you," I said to my mom, rolling my eyes.

"As you should." She shrugged in agreement. "I ate the last éclair five minutes ago." At this, she chuckled heartily over my shoulder and walked out of the room. Smiles escaped my eyes and my mouth.

"*C'est magnifique!*" I repeated to Papaly, clapping my hands.

Daylight was young and danced around my room, tracing the timber floors, bouncing amorously to the pressed mirror in the boudoir. Throwing my hair into its familiar bun, I spun Papaly by the hand. We bumped hips and swirled fantastically, frolicking about, steps out of rhythm and laughter out of tune.

Dawn eased by, like a cool drink. Taking my time, I walked about the backyard, tracing the memory of every bird crowding the happy little birdhouse that hung secure amongst the leaves.

Giddy was an emotion I seldom felt, so at first, I was unsure why my stomach tumbled with butterflies and my cheeks were stuck round and robust from smiling. Eventually, I realized I was more excited about my date with Appoline than I had been for my date with François. I chalked this up to my pure feelings of indifference toward François and my absolutely unruly adoration for coq au vin. I had always been a hungry girl.

Unsure how to pass the time, I sequestered myself outdoors. Utilizing the vast coastline as my personal bedroom left me vulnerable to the winds brushing me by. I had a burning desire to grow into myself, to fill the space in my head and my eyes with the intimacy I had never been allowed to feel before.

For twenty-one years, I had restricted my emotions and experiences, afraid I'd finally feel something strong enough to provoke commitment or pain or a combination of both. I made it all the way through college without a single romantic affair, terrified I wasn't like my mom, terrified I'd feel more than she did. I had always feared that this moment of internalized reckoning would be the point of no return; that once I dove in, I'd forget how to swim. Standing on the loneliest cliff, barren from anything remotely resembling city life, I overlooked the ocean. Its gentle horde of waves rolled from one end of the world to the other.

Holding out my arms, I tried to measure the seas' expanse, knowing damn well I'd never be able to feel the entirety of the weight it holds. With the breeze pulling at my clothes, I stood there a moment longer. I would never be able to comprehend the magnitude of life passing me by, but just for a moment, I begged myself to simply start *feeling* the meaning of promises, especially the broken ones. No longer would I deprive my being of what it wanted.

Tiptoeing lightly around, blushing discreetly, and shying away from evident truths would not be my inevitable future. I wanted more. My soul was finally waking up, and it was famished.

Practicing my newfound talent of cartwheels on the edge of the overhang, I wiped my dirt-encrusted hands against my shorts, realizing my fingernails were grimy. This was possibly the most unkempt part of my façade. An extra leap and bound brought me inland with the roaming seagulls, mollified as well from their time at sea.

Up the hill of rocky terrain, the village courthouse shrugged under its immense shroud of brick layering. Peculiar though it may seem, the courthouse was the singular fixture of town life that rested alone, isolated from the bustling gossip that corrugated through the city streets. If you wanted to confirm a rumor, pry into someone's personal life, or run away with your concubine, you had to specifically seek out the courthouse on the hill. You had to search for your affirmations.

Most days though, its large wooden doors were closed. Villagers preferred to sort through their disputes the old-fashioned way, by ignoring them until all that remained were passive aggressive run-ins at the market.

It was perhaps an inexplicable twist of fate, providence even, that I saw Monsieur and Madame Alarie, heads down, shoulders hunched, leaving the courthouse that morning, for I certainly wasn't seeking them out.

Hiding behind a large oak tree, sticky from sap residue, I ducked my head in between bristles and branches. The Alaries walked jaggedly apart from one another in stifled permanence.

I bit my fingers, anxious and confused by their demeanor. Just as they were about to disappear into the parking lot adjacent to the creaking hall doors, Madame Alarie shouted something, causing Monsieur Alarie to stop mid-step. I could see his chest level in and out from yards away. Slowly, he turned to face Madame Alarie, throwing a pile of papers at her feet before driving away, over the looming hill.

Afraid he had abandoned her to walk all the way home, I crept out from my hiding spot behind the oak. Thankfully, before I called out to Madame Alarie, she approached another car that had been parked next to Monsieur Alarie's. She drove off, following carefully in his tracks. Relief swept over my interrupted breathing. They had taken two separate cars. A miracle.

When I got back to my grandfather's cottage, I found my mom and Appoline sitting cross-legged, splendidly outstretched on the warm mauve couch, knitting and laughing with arms linked. Stumbling over the hearth, I shook the wind from my hair.

"Appoline? What are you doing here?" I paused after this question, realizing I was out of breath and sweaty from my race home.

"Right, sorry." She smiled shyly, the buds of her cheeks beginning to blossom like cherries. "I realize I'm a little early."

"Early? Appoline, dinner is at seven. It's noon."

"Well, I—I was hungry...so I came over early," she faltered.

"I was supposed to meet you in town, though." I countered.

"I'm *very* hungry." Appoline had decided this was her most believable excuse, and I let her have it. "I just couldn't wait," she added bashfully.

Laughing and eyeing her suspiciously, I grabbed some water from the kitchen counter and returned to see my mom comparing her aggregation of woven fabric to Appoline's.

"What are you two even doing?" I asked, gulping down my water and reveling in the fact that I had the upper hand.

Was Appoline nervous...anxious even?

"We're knitting." My mom smiled pleasantly, unaware of the tension in the room.

"I'd hardly call that knitting," I grumbled.

"Bellamy Artois!" Appalled with my candor, my mother folded her arms and gifted me a stern look. "Once you can do better, then you can criticize our work."

"I can't do better, but I have the decency not to even try!" I joked, stealing the yarn from Appoline's hands before mischievously dashing to my bedroom.

Hearing Appoline squeal with delight and embarrassment, I hid quietly in my closet, waiting for her to come find me and playfully steal the yarn back. I was panting heavily as I felt the thump of footsteps shifting over the wood floor.

"Aha!" Appoline threw open the closet door and jumped on top of me, straddling my hips with her legs.

We fought over the yarn for a brief moment, before I gave in and let her glory in an undeserved victory. She was warm and light as she bounced atop me, her thighs brushing against mine. I shuddered.

"You're tickling me!" I pushed her off abruptly and involuntarily. My hands shot to my thighs.

"Bah, calm down, what is your problem?" Appoline asked, laughing at my discomfort.

"Nothing, I'm just sweaty. I need to shower."

To my credit, this wasn't a lie. I was sweaty. Appoline didn't respond. She was lying back in the corner of the closet, her head cushioned by a pile of dirty clothes, her eyes closed. Odd though it seemed, she looked to be tremendously at peace. Annoyed with myself, I bit my tongue for a moment before continuing on.

"Hello? Are you not going to respond with some sort of witty comeback? Tell me showers are pointless and I should go swim in the ocean if I want a true sense of cleanliness. Cleanse ourselves in the cathartic waters of the Atlantic maybe?" I was pacing outside the closet door, waiting for an answer.

"Hmm, you're the poet, Bellamy. But that sounds like a great idea. We should do it," Appoline replied with a lackadaisical hum.

I knew her eyes were still closed by the vulnerable and delicate nature of her voice; I didn't even need to look.

"Ugh, I'm not a poet, I just said what I thought *you* were going to say," I said.

"See, look at that. Writing before my very eyes. You are a talent, Bellamy."

Appoline was dreamy, her head clearly no longer on a pile of my dirty laundry, but instead, somewhere high in the clouds.

"What are you doing in there anyway? Taking a nap?"

I had begun to strip, preparing to shower. My thoughts were moving quickly, and my feet couldn't keep up.

"I like closets..." She drifted back to me for a moment. "They're so calming. Comforting. Come here. Come see."

Appoline's fingers twiddled in the doorway from her spot on the ground. Sighing, I crouched next to her in the narrow closet. Her eyes never opened, unwavering. I took shameful glances at her face, as I made myself comfortable just below her shoulder, cramped in a space meant for one...meant for clothing.

I liked the way she looked; I knew this. Yet, I was afraid of how she would feel. I was afraid of her touch.

Shoulder to shoulder now, I tried desperately to create a sliver of space between our sides. I shimmied artfully beside Appoline, hoping not to disturb her newfound tranquility.

"I've never seen you this calm," I whispered. "Was it the knitting?"

"It's the closet," Appoline said, eyes shut delicately.

She said this with more surety than I had ever heard anyone say anything before.

"It's the closet," I repeated, staring longingly at the ceiling, praying this comfort would never end.

Late afternoon greeted us promptly with earnest laughter drifting amongst the breeze from the kitchen to my bedroom. I had showered and dressed while Appoline indulged, with toes sprawled, in my closet.

Downstairs, we found my mother and grandfather having a grand old time, sipping on absinthe, red in the face from rebellion.

"Are you guys really drinking absinthe?" I smelled the emerald glass bottle before Appoline took it from me, shrugged, and poured herself a glass.

"Yes, Papaly told me it's your favorite," my mom giggled.

"You're not allowed to be drunk yet. The sun is still out. That's sacrilegious. Plus, I'm sober. You can't be drunk before I am." Incredulous yet amused, I grabbed the glass from my grandfather's hand and turned to my mom.

"*Bah, on a des problèmes.*" *We're in trouble*, my grandfather whispered to the group as they burst out laughing.

"You're the adults! I should be the one drinking absinthe in the afternoon, and *you* should be the ones scolding me for it!" I laughed, jealous of the fun they were having without me. All three of them stared at me, slightly concerned.

"Here," Appoline handed her top-heavy tumbler to me. "Now you're drinking at four in the afternoon, too."

"And we won't even scold you for it," my mom added.

"You're a horrible influence. You all are. Especially you!" I pointed to my grandfather.

Papaly, with wide eyes locked on mine, slowly and carefully reached for the bottle, pouring himself more. I didn't say anything. Everyone waited in anticipation. Rolling my eyes, I lifted my tumbler up in the air and chugged its contents with unsettling ease.

"*Voilà!*" Papaly clapped and stood to refill my glass.

We all laughed, green with absinthe and rosy with cheer. I shook my head, eyeing Appoline, who was now complimenting my mom on her awfully knitted sweater.

"*C'est horrible,*" Papaly whispered to me, nodding at the sweater in Appoline's hands.

My mom was gushing, waving her hands around, embarrassed. Laughing, I turned to my grandfather.

"*C'est le pire.*" *It's the worst,* I whispered back to him, giggling as we clinked our glasses together and watched the women we adored ogle drunkenly over an ugly sweater.

Thoroughly buzzed and no longer combative, I was beginning to get hungry and the day-old baguette from Monsieur Fortin's wasn't sufficing. With only a quarter measure of absinthe remaining in the bottle, Appoline, my mother, my grandfather, and I stood surrounding the bread on the center of the table, playing Russian roulette.

"Come on," I tugged at Appoline's waist. "Let's go, I'm hungry."

"Hungry? But dinner isn't until seven, Bellamy," she teased, taking a jab at the comments I had made to her earlier.

"Ugh," I muttered as I squirmed around in my tight jeans and sexy, yet quite uncomfortable, body suit.

"What's wrong with you?" my mom asked.

"I just hate being dressed up. It's such a hassle, and I'm always uncomfortable." I pulled at my jeans.

"Then go change into sweatpants or something," Appoline suggested through a mouthful of bread.

"But we're going to dinner," I complained.

"So? Who cares?" She shrugged her shoulders and simultaneously shoved another large chunk in her mouth.

"We're going up into the fancy part of town, though."

"And? I'll change, too." She smiled at me.

"Really?" I asked, hopeful. "What I would give to eat a large plate of pasta in stretchy pants right now."

"Yeah, come on." Appoline took my hand and dragged me to my bedroom where we both promptly put on my nicest set of pajamas.

"*C'est la vie!*" *Such is life*, I said as we studied ourselves in the mirror. "Let's fucking eat."

//

In the absence of gilded bottles, perennial laughter, and the safety net of familial faces, Appoline and I walked brazenly inland up toward the château on the hill.

"We're going to be an hour early for our reservation," Appoline said, the gravel pavement transitioning to brick as we climbed higher.

"We're hungry girls, we can't help that." I shrugged, smiling at her. "Plus, you know everyone in town. They'll seat us early if you ask them to."

"Using me for my name now?" She winked.

I caught her in step, elbow in my palm.

"What?" Appoline asked.

"Appoline, I'm *really* hungry tonight."

She shrugged. "Your pajamas look better on me than you!" she teased, tickling my palm with her fingers before pulling me up hill.

"That's because you're wearing a set of pearls with yours!" I pointed at the gaudy necklace that I had never seen Appoline wear before.

"Oh, I hate this thing. Mother practically begged me to wear it." She unclasped the pearls and put them around my neck swiftly. "There, now you're set."

I groaned, pulling lightly on the smooth pearls, and hoping my cheeks weren't as red as they felt. She giggled as I struggled to keep up with her fast pace. We arrived at La Lumière, the bistro adjacent to Hôtel Alarie, just as the sun was getting tired, and were promptly greeted with peculiar stares.

Appoline batted her eyelashes at the host, pouting delicately in sultry French until he decided his best option would be to seat us at their nicest table. I could tell he was tired of stumbling over his words, as Appoline rendered him incompetent. Watching Appoline flirt made me uneasy. A pang kicked me in the gut, but I chose to pretend it was due to my hunger and not my irrational jealousy.

Clouded by the absinthe running through our veins, I suggested we order shots of Cointreau before our appetizer. This was met with excited clapping from Appoline. Rather than shy away from recklessness, we welcomed it with open arms, adding gasoline to the beautiful fire we lit before our eyes. It kept our faces warm and dissipated any possible notion of regret.

The waiter looked at us quizzically as I ordered the escargot, so I ordered a bottle of champagne, as well, making sure to flaunt my pajama set as I did. Almost as if he was unsure whether to ask or not, he proceeded to inquire if we were celebrating anything in particular.

"*Oui, oui, oui,*" Appoline babbled quickly, waving her hand at me. "*Un an de sobriété.*" *To a year of sobriety*, she told the waiter with delight.

I reached over and grasped Appoline's hand with compassion.

"I am so proud of you," I said rather convincingly.

She choked back laughter, as we stared admiringly into one another's eyes. Moments later, the waiter had returned with our shots of Cointreau and bottle of champagne.

"*Merci, monsieur.*" Appoline smiled lovingly at the waiter as he scurried off.

"Cheers," I said, swaying happily back and forth.

Appoline and I linked our arms across the table and tipped our heads back, letting the sunset decorate our swelling necks. We sat luxuriously on the balcony of La Lumière, allowing all of life to erupt around us.

"*Madame désire les pâtes.*" *The lady will have the pasta.* I said this to the waiter just as Appoline had taught me to mere moments before. She gave me a thumbs-up. Hearing her laugh with pleasure made my cheeks redden.

"*Et, madame désire le coq au vin.*" *And the lady will have the coq au vin.* Appoline in turn, ordered for me. We guffawed with elevated pompousness.

"Was that good?" I asked hopefully, leaning in as the waiter walked away.

"*C'était parfait.*" *It was perfect*, she said, and blew me a kiss.

"I mustered every ounce of French blood in me trying not to stutter," I laughed.

"Bah, don't admit that to me! Pretend you knew what you were doing all along. It's what I do," she joked.

"You speak fluent French," I responded.

"*Oui, mais,* sometimes I forget."

I paused for a moment. The waiter returned with two more shots of Cointreau. I picked mine up quickly, shooting it back and setting it down aggressively in front of Appoline.

"Rumor has it, you like me," I blurted out.

"Who told you that?" Appoline didn't miss a beat, sipping her Cointreau with refinement, then placing the empty glass next to mine.

Checkmate.

"Your boyfriend," I said slyly.

"Which one?"

"The one you didn't want to sleep with yesterday."

"You should get your news from a more reliable source." Appoline leveled her eyes, not giving anything away.

"I'd say he's the most reliable source there is."

Standstill. The wind stopped briefly and the potted flowers on the edge of the balcony wilted with uncertainty. Ahead of us, the sky stretched to the cliffs, clouds floating out to sea purely of their own volition.

"And Bellamy...if the rumor was true? Then what?" Appoline held my gaze, refusing to back down.

My stomach rolled with anxiety. Her collarbones, smooth and pointed, jutted out from her sternum. She tilted her head slightly, allowing her endless cascade of black hair to fall across her face.

I couldn't tell if she was asking the question to poke fun at my insistence, or to see if I'd actually reveal how badly I wanted to push back her hair and lick her neck right there on the restaurant balcony for all to see.

I shook my head, embarrassed and afraid she could read the thoughts fleeting across my face. She must be taunting me.

"Désolée." Sorry. "I didn't mean..." My voice trailed off as the waiter returned with my coq au vin and Appoline's plate of tiered pasta.

"Monsieur," Appoline reached out, grabbing the waiter by the elbow. *"Un verre de vin rouge, pour madame." A glass of red wine, for the lady.* She nodded in my direction as she said this.

"Et, un verre de vin blanc, pour madame." And a glass of white wine, for the lady, I added quietly, and with much less confidence than before.

Neither of us spoke until the waiter returned with our wine.

"You know, I haven't heard any rumors about *you* liking *me*," Appoline stated with clarity.

"That's because I'm better at keeping secrets than you are," I said pointedly, the rush of alcohol steeping into my brain.

"Oh, is that so?" She laughed. "You have no idea the things you don't know about me."

When she said this, she raised her eyebrows playfully. I took this gesture as a lighthearted truce.

Lifting my wine glass to hers, I cleared my throat. "To rumors."

Appoline liked this. "To rumors," she repeated.

Diving benevolently into our food, the two of us indulged in the evening, gifted with the best table in the house, bitter wine, and the soft looks we gave one another; restless and unspoken confessions sat between us.

It wasn't until my second glass of wine and empty plate that I realized Appoline had barely touched her pasta at all. In my best attempt not to slur my words, I asked her if I could finish it off.

"Please, I'm not very hungry." She pushed her plate toward me.

The pasta was a creamy concoction of butter and sage that melted on my tongue. Eagerly, I shoved the noodles into my mouth, incomprehensibly insatiable. Appoline watched with intent, teasing her wine glass with her plump, sensuous lips.

"You're ravenous," she said, drinking me in.

"My stomach is like a bottomless pit," I said through thick mouthfuls.

"Strange. I'm never hungry when I'm with you," Appoline sighed.

"You've said that before," I reminded her.

"I just want to make sure I'm getting my point across," she answered smoothly.

I looked up, mouth still full of heavy cream. "Then why did we come out to dinner?"

"Because *you're* always hungry," she replied, licking the red stains from her lips and waving at the waiter for another glass of wine.

"Well, consumption is my favorite pastime." I chewed thoughtfully.

Moments later, we were dashing down the pavement once again, moonlight leading the way. Dinner had ended, but we were wide awake now. Paul Simon's "For Emily, Whenever I May Find Her" had been playing at La Lumière, and neither one of us could get it out of our heads. We sang to one another.

"What a dream I had..."

"Pressed in organdy..."

"Wait, who's Emily?"

"What?" Appoline skipped down the path, humming under her breath.

"The song. It's called For Emily, Whenever, or is it wherever? I'm not sure... Wherever I May Find Her," I explained, thinking more scrupulously than intended.

Wine seemed to always have one of two effects on me. Either it made me exuberant and careless, or unnecessarily methodical and sardonic.

"*Je ne sais pas* who the hell Emily is, but she clearly had some kind of pull. Getting people to wander..." Her voice trailed as she looked at me, kicking pebbles with her foot.

"Empty streets down..." I sang, as she joined me in unbridled harmony.

"Past the shop displays."

I laughed as we each held our breath for a brief moment of stoic suspension.

"We're awful singers," I admitted.

Appoline turned to take the path back into town.

"Hey, wait. Let's go to the hotel...you never want to take me there." I nodded up toward the hill where we had just come from.

"I don't want to take *anyone* there. Why do you always want to go there so badly?" She rolled her eyes.

"Why *don't* you want to go there so badly? What are you hiding?" I eyed her suspiciously.

"Ugh, nothing. It's just..."

"It's just what?" I whined. "You want to sleep at the dock again? Or do you want to sleep like queens in a white satin bed with room service?" I stretched my arms wide, twirling with the breeze.

The wine had been relatively potent.

"You can be quite annoying, you know that?" Appoline was getting antsy. "Wait, first, I have a surprise."

"If you're taking me to the pub again, Appoline…"

"No, I'm not feeding you anymore alcohol. You can barely stand as it is."

"Hey, I'd say I'm faring pretty well for the amount of liquor that's been circulating my body."

"Yeah," she scoffed. "It's all that pasta that's soaking it up."

"I wasn't going to let it go to waste!" I wrapped my arms around her hips, hanging onto her, allowing the liquor to have its way.

"Come on." Appoline ushered me forward as she escaped from my grasp.

"Mean," I muttered, eyes to the ground.

"You need a pick me up," she said.

I pouted and crossed my arms.

"You're being a baby." Swiftly, Appoline slipped her arm around my waist, drawing me close.

"I know." I nodded happily. "But I'm trying to get my way."

"Be my Emily," Appoline whispered in a rushed tone of fervor.

"What?"

"Be my Emily…wander with me…please?" She said this last word as though its very existence was causing her great pain.

"I can't be your Emily," I stated cleanly, my mind foggier than my tongue. "We haven't found her yet."

Appoline pinched the skin above my ribs in reply, but I didn't mind. I was just thankful she was holding me. Understanding this was as compliant as I'd be, Appoline took her chance to steer us south.

Wobbling our way into the village, I fought the urge to slip Appoline's hand under my shirt. It rested safely just below my breast, and I wasn't sure if I was imagining it, but a few times, I was almost certain her fingers twitched, grazing the underwire of my bra.

Concerned that I was clearly grasping at straws and confused as to why I even craved her touch so immovably, I stayed clear of making any rash decisions, allowing Appoline to simply take me for a walk, just as she had desired.

When we got to the cul-de-sac in the center of town, she let go of my waist and moved behind me, covering my eyes with both of her hands.

"Appoline, I'm not sure if you know this, but drunk people don't fare well in general, let alone when they can't see."

I could feel her chest against my back, her excited strokes of breath nicking my neck.

"Et, voilà!" she screamed with delight as she released her hands from my face and spun me around.

"Spinning a drunk person hasn't been proven to help either." I laughed, woozy from the day's binging and grabbing her shoulders to steady myself.

L'Écume de la Mer, the creamery of my childhood, stood brilliantly aloof amongst its only counterpart, the black sky. The twinkling decorations flushed the air with the smell of cherries and blossoming nostalgia. Painted pink, this village establishment slumped colorfully downhill, the cobblestone road in front, illuminated solely by streetlamps and the renowned glowing ten-foot freezer.

"Appoline," I slurred with knowing glee. "You can't even deny that you like me now."

Rolling her eyes, she pulled me into the shop, where I had basked many years before in the exotic flavors of French ice cream. Flashes of sticky nights, wild and sweaty, returned to me instantly. Leisurely careless summers accompanied by bounding restlessness wavered as I stood at the counter, a twelve-year-old again, attempting to make the biggest decision of her life.

"I don't know what to get," I said, beginning to feel overwhelmed.

"You're allowed any flavor, but make it fun, remember. Those are the rules."

Appoline was clearly recalling the evenings we spent as children, passing time here.

"Blood orange," I said distinctly, staring directly into the eyes of the man behind the counter.

I swayed, and Appoline steadied me with her hip against mine.

"Yes!" she screamed in encouragement. "Another one!"

"What?" I turned to her, almost dropping the blood orange custard melting quickly and lewdly down my hand.

"I owe you for like seven birthdays. Pick a few more flavors, Bellamy. We're going to celebrate each year you missed. We have to make up for lost time." She smiled at me brightly, her eyes gliding over my lips, covered in silky frozen custard. "And then, you're never going to miss another birthday with me ever again," Appoline winked.

Every unintended salacious moment up to this point, I had ignored. My mind had been wandering to places it wasn't invited to, and I was quick to retract, afraid I'd push Appoline away with my eagerness. She had made it very clear she wasn't interested in the intimacy I was craving to give her.

Holding back made my fingers clench and stomach patter, yet, for some reason, when she told me to order more ice cream, I knew it was because she wanted an excuse to share. Appoline desired my taste in her mouth. That was clear, it had to be.

Reading into this far too much, I ordered the flavors I recalled were her favorite from our youth: raspberry, white chocolate peach. Gluttonously, we stumbled out of the creamery, swapping custard cones as I attempted desperately to ignore her amorous licking. She knew what she was doing when her gaze met mine, tongue full of cold dessert, hungry for anything sweet and delicate.

Scattered footsteps and dancing winds led us to the stone bench that rested happily cracked beneath the only two streetlamps in the cul-de-sac, with lights dim enough to expose the night fog.

"*Bon anniversaire, Bellamy.*" *Happy birthday*, Appoline whispered as we tipped our two ice cream cones together in an effort to cheers.

"Hey, you got raspberry on my orange." I laughed uneasily, all of a sudden nervous with the energy I had manifested before us.

Appoline raised her eyebrows. "They taste good mixed together, though."

"I do like trying new things." My feet dangled, our ankles kissing below us. Swarming in self-awareness, I watched the butterflies in my stomach tumble from my lips to fly away, wings spread and quivering. I wore liquor as a coated armor and leaned in, letting Appoline observe as I bit my lip.

"One out of ten, what do you think are the chances that we kiss before the summer is over?" I asked.

To my drunken delight, Appoline didn't seem taken aback in the slightest by my intrusive insistence.

"Bellamy, not everything has to be as deep as you make it. Some things don't have to be a moment, they can just be part of one." She laughed at me, licking her ice cream, unbothered and oblivious to the moment she had just created herself.

Resigned, but not yet discouraged, I turned to the second ice cream cone in my hand, catching drops of liquid sugar in my mouth, my head tilted upside down.

"Are you going to share?" Appoline nudged me gently, prodding her elbow into my side.

Reluctantly, I held the white chocolate peach custard in front of her face, expecting her to grab it from me greedily. Instead, she sat there, swinging her legs back and forth, licking the ice cream from the cone in my hand.

"Do you like eating from the palms of my hands, Appoline?" I asked.

"Hush. I'm trying to enjoy myself," she giggled.

Feeling frivolous and full of tipsy merriment, I shoved the ice cream gently into Appoline's face, just as she was leaning forward for more. She shrieked with surprise, turning to me in awe.

"What?" I shrugged, smiling slyly. "It slipped."

Quickly in retaliation, Appoline dug her fingers into the custard and reached over, smearing it across my lips. Giggling, I obliged, letting her sticky fingers trace down my bottom lip, tickling my chin.

Sticking my tongue out, I licked my lips, inviting Appoline to stay. Her thumb brushed the corner of my mouth, and I closed my lips around it. She didn't pull away. Foreheads bent together, I stared deeply into her face, avoiding her eyes. It would have been too much.

"Ten," Appoline whispered.

"What?"

"Ten," she repeated, pulling her thumb from my mouth and bringing it to her own. "Chances are a ten."

She sucked on it, while watching me bite my lip in nervous anticipation. With custard smeared on both of our faces, Appoline leaned in, kissing me gently, white chocolate peach dripping down our necks.

The ice cream cone dropped from my hand to the ground between our feet and I made no attempt to save it. Grasping my neck with her hands, Appoline pulled me into her, devouring my taste. She pressed her tongue into my mouth, becoming the aggressor that I had always pictured I would be.

Shaking and unsure what to do with myself, I let Appoline take my hand in hers, bringing it up to her sternum and dragging it down her chest. I paused, no longer certain what she wanted from me.

As she pulled her head away from mine, she wiped at the white saliva that stretched across her mouth. Then, she wiped mine. We sat there in silence, the night wrapping around our bodies, glowing only from the streetlamps and moonlight.

My chest was pattering incessantly, as I waited for her to kiss me again. Her lips were soft and sweet, yet her hands around my throat made me yearn for submission. I wanted her on me, over me, in me.

"You dropped the ice cream," Appoline pointed out.

Hearing her speak, after her mouth had just been pressed against mine, made my thighs tingle. She sounded different. Impulsively, and without answering, I slid my hand around her hip, drawing her near. My leg collapsed on top of hers, my fingers in the band of her pants, brushing skin. I licked her neck, just as I had desired to do so at the restaurant, and she let me.

Feeling Appoline's reciprocation made me ravenous. I bit her neck lightly and then returned to her mouth, hungry for her smell, her presence. It took everything in me not to bite her lips, plump and garrulous between mine. Sneaking my fingers down her pant leg, I clawed at the heat created from our sweat and desire.

Almost instantly, Appoline tugged on my hair, roughly pulling my head back and away from her face.

I was out of breath, eagerly waiting for her release, so I could venture my hand away from her thigh and closer to the warmth, itching to feel her tremble.

"Let's go back to the hotel," she whispered blatantly, cheeks flushed and eyes adamant.

"You're going to take me back there?" I finally spoke, my voice cracking.

"Isn't that what you've been begging for?" She smiled.

"I've been begging for a lot of things," I admitted bashfully.

"I know. Well, this one I'm giving you." Appoline rose from the bench, the glimmering from the lights above reflecting on her opaque mane of hair.

"Come on." She held out her hand.

"I'm sticky," I said, hesitating.

"So am I."

"Well, I guess I am your Emily," I conceded.

"Well, I guess you are," Appoline agreed.

Chapter Fourteen

SEPARATE FROM THE COLIC haunting me the entirety of the summer, I threw up behind the bushes stapled pristinely before the lobby of Hôtel Alarie. While I knew I would be embarrassed by my inability to stay collected come the morning, my head was spinning too fast for last minute insecurities to realign my judgment.

Appoline and I had sprinted all the way back uptown, stopping only once to admire the wooden birdhouse hanging in my grandfather's backyard. Pointing gaily and with blissful, sleepy eyes, I told her it had been my good omen.

"For what did you need a good omen?" she asked when we began racing past the browned, tapering fence along the outskirts of Papaly's land.

"I didn't say I needed one." My arms began to weigh down my heaving body. "It just presented itself to me this morning. I knew it was going to be a good day."

"The birds chirp every morning, Bellamy," Appoline noted with terse laughter.

The two of us were jogging toward the footbridge that corked its way over a valley of slimy pebbles below.

"Well, this was the first morning that I noticed them." I staggered my breathing just as I was taught to do during cross-country practice.

After I had finished puking up the remains of Appoline's tiered pasta, I bashfully suggested I go back to my grandfather's.

"Aw, *ma chérie*. Come on." She rubbed my back, ensuring that any confidence I had gained throughout the evening was lost swiftly and easily.

When we arrived at her fourth-floor suite, we stood on our heels, bobbing side to side. Finally, we broke the barrier, stepping over the threshold and allowing the night to continue exuding its inertia of bubbling energy, from my chest to hers.

After drawing a bath for me, Appoline slipped out of the marbled bathroom and closed the door behind her quickly, being as polite and respectful as possible. Sliding into the abstract life of the Renaissance painting hanging above the sink, I plunged my head underwater, begging not only for release but for absolution.

Grandiose, with tufts of silk wrapped neatly around her head, jewels pinned eloquently in her hair, the woman in the painting was soft, yet regal. She lay at ease in a bed of beautifully warm fabric, her back to me, but her face turned, peering gently over her shoulder. Naked and unaware, or maybe naked and beautifully bold, the woman's spine curved, elongating the expanse from her shoulders to her hips. Her arm covered her breasts and the bedsheets splayed perfectly over her bottom. She knew I was looking at her, admiring her smooth skin, enchanting the world with mystery and desire.

I laughed to myself, emerging from the water. The painted woman wasn't smiling, but she wasn't sad; she was just aware.

Wrapped securely in the white hotel robe that had hung in the bathroom, I walked into the suite to find Appoline sitting cross-legged on the bed, a pot of tea beside her and bread on the nightstand. Without speaking, I crawled into bed close to her, the cotton blankets pronounced and inspired, just as I remembered them from my youth. After pouring me a cup of tea, Appoline ripped a piece of bread off the baguette. I ate and drank what she'd offered me in silence.

Stomach warm with comfort, I turned on my side, my back away from Appoline. Sleepily, I discarded my robe, letting it fall to the floor and reveal my freshly washed façade. I wanted to be the woman in the painting. Failing to peek over my naked shoulder, my eyes drifted shut as I collapsed into a dark slumber, Appoline's fingers running up and down my back until I couldn't feel any longer.

As sun creaked delightfully into the hotel suite, raining streaks of light across my eyelids, I stirred peacefully. I remembered where I was before remembering why. Rolling over, I stretched my arms above my head and realized I was wrapped in the robe I had cast off just hours before.

Appoline wasn't in bed with me, so I immediately rose, stepping gently over the waste basket that she must have set beside the bed after I had fallen asleep. The room was much more majestic in the morning dew. Crown moldings and tastefully varnished wood furniture decorated the already crisp ambience, golden sparkles of ethereal rainbows glinting the walls.

Amidst the pallor of the marbled floors and the persistent calm of the space from here to there, I squinted, seeing feet splayed in disarray, sticking out of the walk-in closet. More concerned than confused, I pulled open the doors to reveal Appoline, asleep on the floor, a pillow resting gracefully under her head, her knees tucked up to her chin. Crawling beside her, I nestled my cheek on her back. Groggily, Appoline yawned and opened her eyes.

"You just couldn't stand the idea of sharing a bed with me, huh?" I joked quietly.

The corners of her mouth twitched upward with affection.

"It just feels so...safe...down here," she whispered.

Holding her in my arms now, I kissed her shoulder blade.

"Thank you for taking care of me last night," I said.

"Thank you for only throwing up once," Appoline replied.

Her tangle of black hair shaded my face, as she let me cuddle her on the floor of the closet, a mess of khaki pants hanging above us. With the previous night's custard kisses still vibrant in my memory, I quietly traced the curve of her waist to her hip with my forefinger, fluttering when I got to her thigh. Slowly, I pressed my body against hers, moving my hand inward toward her pelvis.

I paused, then began kissing her neck, biting it lightly as I stroked the hair away from her face. Bringing my hand up her inner thigh, to her stomach, I slipped under her shirt, finally caressing her breasts the way I had imagined the day I'd accidentally brushed against her by the dock. Appoline groaned and I took this as a positive. Her body relaxed into mine and I pulled her even closer, my legs wrapped around hers.

No longer hesitant, I circled her nipples with my fingers until they were hard, then pinched them lightly, sucking on her neck with unjustifiable passion. I was sure she could feel the pulse in between my legs, beating rapidly against her.

"Bellamy," she moaned.

"Yeah. Say my name again." I had never been so eager and excited in my life. Lust was taking over my mind and my ears.

"No, Bellamy. Stop, hold on." Appoline pulled her neck away from my mouth, and it took everything in me not to grab her throat and bring her back toward me.

"What? What's wrong?" I asked, my hand still holding her breast tightly.

"Not...not in the closet," she said.

Quickly, she removed herself from me, sitting up and rubbing her temples. I was breathing heavily, a leech exposed to blood for the first time. Appoline stood and walked over to the bed, sitting down in contemplation. Following her lead, I jumped atop her, straddling her hips with my legs, and pushing her down on the bed.

My lips met hers as my hands tried to tear her shirt off over her head.

"Bellamy, stop." Appoline pushed at my shoulders and rolled out from under me.

Confused and concerned that I had come on too strong, I sat frozen, unsure what to do.

"I—I'm sorry..." I stuttered.

Appoline rolled her eyes, making me even more nervous. Tears welled up in the corners of mine.

"I thought...I can't figure out what you want, Appoline. You kissed *me* last night! And you took me back here, and now...now you..."

"What do *you* want?" Appoline turned quickly, slapping me in the face with words as sharp as stone.

I stared at her, hoping the stern look sewn tightly in her eyebrows would soon disappear. Suddenly, and before I had a chance to answer, Appoline's hand was around my throat. She took me by surprise, pushing me down on the bed just roughly enough. My eyes widened. She smiled greedily, taking her other hand and aggressively tearing open my robe.

"Is this what you want?" she whispered, staring me straight in the eyes, fingers stroking just underneath my bellybutton.

Her gaze never left my face, but I knew she could feel the goosebumps that had arisen down my spine.

I nodded, her hand a necklace on my throat. Sighing, she released her grip and fell down next to me. Staring at the ceiling and avoiding one another's confusion, we sunk into the bed.

"We can't, Bellamy," Appoline said finally.

"Why not?" I murmured, tying my robe once again, embarrassed.

"It isn't right. You're inexperienced, and I remembered that when you were throwing up last night."

"I'm twenty-one," I said.

"And I'm twenty-four, but that's not the point. The point is it will ruin everything."

"But I want to." My voice cracked, and I knew I sounded vulnerable, but it didn't matter anymore. There was no reason to put up a front. "I thought maybe you wanted to," I reasoned with her.

Appoline chuckled lightly. "Then what? Are you going to remember to leave before I wake up in the morning?"

"Of course," I giggled. "I know the rules."

Appoline tugged at the belt of my robe, clearly considering.

"Let's just see what happens," she decided, pulling me in close and kissing me with the longing that I had felt she was holding in, hiding from me in the light of day.

Appoline and I kissed, her lips running down my neck, my hands on her back, dining on her smell of citrus and taste of melon.

"Well, that didn't take a lot of convincing," I joked.

"Shut up." When she tucked her hand inside the breast of my robe, suddenly I felt bare and exposed. I shivered.

"It's bright in here," I mentioned, caressing her cheek and grazing it lightly with mine.

"So?" Distracted, she worked her way down the cusp of my breast, brushing my sternum and tickling my ribs.

"It...it was darker in the closet," I gulped lightly, yet continued on despite being ignored by Appoline. "It was easier."

"What?" She stopped and looked at me.

"In the dark, it was easier," I said honestly.

"Oh, now you want to be shy?" Appoline teased.

I smiled at her, holding her chin in my hands. For the first time since we had kissed with melted ice cream running down our cheeks, I looked at her purposefully, intently in the eyes. She was restless and didn't want to be stared at for too long. Three knocks at the door told us breakfast had arrived, and begrudgingly, I rolled over.

Appoline bounded to the door as I tied my robe. She returned hastily with a meal fit only for someone who had spent the night in a white cotton bed the night before. Eagerly, she placed all the food out on the comforter, buttering her toast with an excitement I had never seen from her before.

A baguette, a loaf of brioche, a quiche with ham twisted atop, a bowl of strawberries, and a chocolate croissant sat before me on a white and blue platter. I was a queen, presented with a feast, but I sipped my espresso instead and watched Appoline bounce with joy. In two fleeting moments, she had polished off half of the baguette.

"I've never seen you eat this much," I laughed, truly intrigued.

"I've never been this hungry," she said, shrugging.

I didn't reply.

"Hey," Appoline eyed me suspiciously. "Don't get all weird."

She threw a piece of bread at my face, giggling.

"I'm just surprised you haven't had a mimosa yet," I said, stealing the chocolate croissant from her hands and taking a ravenous bite.

"Oh, darling." Appoline stood, luxury held in the nuance of her walk. "What do you think these are for?"

She pulled out two champagne glasses from the bar by the sofa, laughing with sweetened ease, her cheeks warm and happy.

The morning lumbered on as we devoured our breakfast, just waiting to be satiated. Personally, I suspected the pit in my stomach might never be truly full. Singular pauses of brief uncertainty rounded out the cricks in our conversation, reminding us that we were human, and time was fleeting. Moments that I had waited so long for had come and gone, leaving me to accept that I'd never feel exactly the same way as I had when Appoline's custard covered lips first touched mine, ever again.

I caught myself chuckling lightly, just as I had the night before, while emerging dramatically and seamlessly from the bathtub. The lapses in dialogue had my mind wandering, and I couldn't help but wonder when I had grown so overly sentimental, or better yet, emotionally overbearing.

It happened. New things will always happen, until we stop being a part of time. What was I so afraid of? Acknowledging the discussion in my head made me laugh more. Appoline smiled, pouring me another glass of champagne accessorized with orange juice.

"Are you drunk or just talking to yourself?" she asked.

"The day feels lemony," I stated, not answering her question in any sense.

"So, drunk," she noted cheekily. "Come on. Get dressed."

"All I have are my pajamas."

"Great, then put those on."

With streaks of intoxication blurring my vision, Appoline and I ran rampant in the halls of the hotel, stealing the housekeeping cart from the maid's closet. Appoline had made several copies of the key. We laughed as I threw toilet paper over door handles and she slipped mini-soaps to all the even-numbered rooms.

Appoline sprinted jaggedly as she pushed me down the hall on the cart, a fairy flicking baby powder in the air with one hand and sipping from a champagne glass with the other. We had it all.

From the balcony back in Appoline's suite, we looked out on buttery swarms of melting light scoring the slats of the rooftop. The afternoon salt had shifted from the sea to the wind and traced its way back inland, to the Hôtel Alarie.

Arms spread wide, I inhaled the moment, positive I'd never get to steal a custodial cart in a five-star hotel ever again.

"I want to scream," I mumbled, a baguette aggressively held hostage in my hand.

I was chewing thoughtfully, allowing the Atlantic to weave its way into my mouth, when Appoline howled, beckoning the sun.

As if she was summoned, Muriel came around, banging on the door and bursting into the suite just moments later.

In rapid French, Muriel held up armfuls of toilet paper and scolded Appoline, who giggled at being caught. The pair spoke with vigor, but it was clear that Muriel had nothing but affection for Appoline. As Muriel hounded her for all the missing soaps, Appoline breezily handed her a mimosa, telling her to calm down.

Gathering that I was intruding on their conversation, I collected my things and kissed Appoline's cheek goodbye, explaining I had to head home. Muriel crossed her arms when she saw me, but I gave her a kiss anyway, ruffling her poufy hair that was full of doubts about my company.

Jubilant peace was echoing ardently through my ears as I meandered aimlessly back to my grandfather's cottage, another afternoon slipping away. Unintentional pockets of melancholic stupors drifted over my shoulders, afraid to skip along with me but still persistent in their presence.

Papaly was gardening when I got home, tending to the bed of budding flowers beyond the overgrown brush of crabgrass. Rosemary and irises had blossomed and were woven together, each holding the other up like friends who dare enjoy kissing, just as much as sprouting.

Meekly, I tiptoed past Papaly's turned back, jumping through my bedroom bay windows, which I had left ajar for the entirety of my stay in Saint __ de Vie. Swiftly and precariously, I landed atop a bed that felt much lumpier than how I had left it.

"*Bah! Merde!*" my mom cursed from beneath my splay of cobbled limbs.

"*Bah, merde* to you too," I said sardonically.

"Bellamy!" My mom had to act incredulous to keep up the façade (for whom I was never sure) that she didn't allow her daughter to swear. It was one of the only put-ons she engaged in and never relented from.

"Well, what the—what are you doing in here?" I asked, rolling over as she popped her head up from the pillow she had squished beneath her.

"Sometimes I come in here," she mumbled, laughing as she caught a view of my face. "This used to be my room, you know."

I held my hands to my head, bracing for a headache.

"You're drunk." My mom was smiling from ear to ear as she spoke.

"No, I'm hungover," I corrected her.

Leaning in, she sniffed me. "No, you're drunk, *mon bébé*. What is that? Champagne?"

"How did you know?" I asked.

"It's eleven in the morning. If it were anything else, I'd be concerned."

"Well, when in Rome, right?" I responded sluggishly, my eyes closing without permission.

"So." My mom turned on her side, propping her head up with her hand. "How was last night?"

"What are you doing?" I was very aware my monochromatic responses were in line with my mood and demeanor, but my mother was not picking up on any of these context clues.

"I'm just checking in! What did you guys do? What did you get to eat? Where did you spend the night?"

She was giddy, a fourteen-year-old excited to gossip.

"Where do you think I spent the night? The dock?" I joked, but kicked myself subtly when I realized that wasn't as wild a concept as it may have seemed to me before.

"You're my only child, Bellamy, am I not allowed to ask about your night?" She exhaled, making me realize she was about to begin a tangent. "You go out, drink, party, and who knows what you do? You stay out all night, you could be selling yourself for all I know!"

Thrusting a pillow completely over my face, I sighed.

"We ate coq au vin and pasta, got ice cream in town, and slept at the hotel."

Though she didn't say anything, I could tell by her silence that she was happy I had decided to share.

"I didn't sell myself until this morning, in case you were wondering," I joked.

At this, my mother stood and pulled the pillow from my face.

"Good, at least I taught you right," she replied.

After kissing me affectionately on the forehead, she turned and walked toward the door.

"What? That's it?" I called after her. "You're done with the interrogation?"

"I'm glad you had fun." She smiled sweetly. "And stop making Muriel upset! That poor woman is old."

"How did you know?" I sat up quickly.

"Appoline's mom called. You're a nuisance, my dear!"

And with that, she swept out of my bedroom to leave me alone with my contemplations and the dwindling afternoon.

//

Swollen and unkempt, I awoke to a stormy cottage, bleak thunder hounding the shutters that hadn't been used for anything other than decorative purposes for years. Gathering myself and draping a blanket around my shoulders, I made my way to the kitchen, where I found my mother and grandfather sipping tea.

A fire crackled in the mud-packed fireplace across the sofa, glowing bright enough to light up the entire room. Above the kitchen nook, the skylights held together by wooden beams were bearing the brunt of the storm howling outside.

It was unclear whether the grey skies that were colluding overhead were a result of the swelling night or the raging squall. Either way, the kitchen emanated a dreary comfort that only a seaside lodge stacked with mugs and pots and woolen knits could bring.

On the dinette, a slew of yarn lay beside a bundle of multicolored macarons. The windchime of seashells dangled angelically in the corner, a decorative piece that brought soft clinks of consolation throughout the night.

"We never have macarons?" I spoke, catching the attention of my family who, up until this point, had no idea I had meandered into the kitchen.

My grandfather smiled approvingly when he heard my stomach growl, standing to serve me a bowl of warm soup that had been simmering on the stove.

"Tiens," Here, he said as he scooted over to make room for me to sit beside him in the booth by the windows.

"How did you sleep, my darling?" My mom was knitting contentedly, a warm loaf of bread placed before her.

"Good, I think."

The carrot soup was seasoned with coriander and cumin, a subtle spice to a sweet dish.

"I haven't seen a storm like this in forever." I swallowed. "It's refreshing."

A snarl of thunder hit the windows, causing the mugs on the table to shake with empathy. I braced myself, shocked by the hit. My mom and grandfather on the other hand, looked unperturbed by the chaos erupting around. In one fell swoop, my mother wiped the spill with a towel and my grandfather refilled their mugs with boiling water from the kettle. Neither of them even moved from their seats.

"It's been happening all night," my mom said, sensing my astonishment.

I laughed, adoration bubbling in my chest.

"What time is it?" I asked, realizing I had no concept of what day it was.

"Um, about half-past eight," a deep voice answered from the hallway.

Jumping from my seat with more fear than when the thunder struck, I saw a brawny figure standing just outside the bathroom. Coming into the light, François chuckled at the look on my face.

"Bonsoir, Bellamy," he said smoothly, leaning in and kissing me on both cheeks.

"So, that's where the macarons came from," I said, adding things up.

"Oui, I brought some over. It's been a while, so I wanted to stop by and see how your mom and grandfather have been doing." He chuckled. "And of course, you."

I looked at my mother and grandfather incredulously, but they both turned their heads, all of a sudden extremely attentive to the week-old newspaper spread on the table. Taking my hand, François ushered me into the living room, where we sat tensely on the sofa. Sweat beaded above my lip from the flames flickering in the air and leaving shadows on the walls.

When François spoke, his voice was level and certain. There was no doubt at all that he knew what he wanted, and he had no issue making it obvious. He was handsome and rugged, and although I had seen him just a few days prior, he looked like a stranger to me now.

"I can't stop thinking about the other night," François said, his voice low and head bent away from the kitchen.

Chewing on a ginger macaron I had snagged from the counter, I squinted at him, unsure what he was referring to. The other night, I was wrapped in a drunken frenzy of beginnings and finalities, Appoline's touch tattooed on my skin, a painted woman watching over me.

"Listen, I know you were nervous, and I didn't want to pressure you, but you left so early in the morning that we didn't even get a chance to talk." François' fingers lightly circled the space in between my shoulder blades, and I shivered with unease.

"Oh, it's okay, don't even worry about it." I blushed, recalling the dissonance that occurred between him and I, her and I, and myself and I, after him and I almost, but didn't, sleep together.

"Well, I'm not worried, so much as I'm impatient," François whispered as lightning struck and lit up my face.

My eyes widened. Nervously, I laughed, shoving the remainder of the macaron in my mouth, hoping this would buy me time to think.

"Impatient?"

"Sorry. I'm just eager to spend more time with you," he corrected himself.

François was so bold and honest that I was beginning to question whether anyone else on Earth truly liked me as much as he did. He was so loud.

Maybe everyone else was just quieter. Whether my cheeks were warm from the fire or the carrot soup, François decided it was because I couldn't hide my embarrassment.

"You're so cute when you blush," he said, crowding my space with his breadth, wide and attentive. "Anyway, I'd really like to take you out again. Maybe next weekend?"

"Next weekend is my birthday," I said, more as a statement to myself than to him.

"Oh, well, looks like we have celebrations in order."

I smiled affectionately and leaned my head on his shoulder, taking him by surprise. The comfort of having someone so fully engaged was easy on my conscience.

"Anyway, I think Carlo and Appoline and I are all meeting up for the festival tomorrow night. I'm assuming you're going?" François relaxed, shirt rustling from his attempt to speak while not disturbing the ebb and flow of his breathing.

"What festival?" I asked.

"*La Fête des Baleines.* Roughly translated as the Festival of Whales. Louie started it a few years ago as a way to sell this absolutely awful liquor he had a full shelf of, and it stuck. Apparently, the drunks in this town have lost their taste from all their time at sea. Now, the village gathers outside his pub for a night of drinking and games and music. Every year, Louie sells his worst liquor for a franc a shot. Really gets morale going."

He was tapping his fingers fluidly on the arm of the sofa, anything to keep from touching me.

"Hm," I said, smelling butter and cognac on François' neck. "I'll be there."

Chapter Fifteen

SWELTERING IN THE RESIDUE of midsummer storms and the humidity that follows angry rainfall, I trailed behind my grandfather adamantly, early afternoon tea brewing. He was pretending not to hear my nagging over the record player that was humming another light and airy Paul Simon tune. Papaly sipped his tea, waving his hand like a maestro.

"Papaly, s'il te plaît!" I cornered him by the stove as he pointed over my shoulder, a feeble attempt to distract me.

Papaly was using any excuse to get out of accompanying me to the Festival of Whales. He mustered a cough, explaining he must've caught a cold. Gin is warm, I told him with arms crossed, it will fix that in no time.

Ah, but no, he had too much cleaning to do. Papaly looked at the kitchen in guilt when he said this. The counters were sparkling and the windows clearer than most anyone's heart.

The only thing out of place was a ladle that had fallen from its spot above the stove. Picking it up, I hung it overhead, turned back to my grandfather, and stood with my hands on my hips. Sighing, he complained about not having anything nice to wear.

"Mais, bien sûr!" But of course! I exclaimed.

In moments, Papaly was wearing his nicest white-striped shirt, a light vest, and his favorite walrus hat. It was about time he made a reintroduction into society; I was sure of it.

When my mom decided to join us at the kitchen nook, we hurrahed, each taking a small, but necessary, shot of Cointreau to start off our evening. Calcified monuments of burly fishermen were etched into the gravel tracks that carried us into town. I remember Papaly fidgeting with his vest as we neared the growing crowd of villagers outside La Baleine Bleue.

The Festival of Whales was much kitschier than I was expecting, especially considering its venue was voted one of France's most picturesque harbors.

Seldom did Papaly venture out to socialize. His only exceptions were for Saul at the winery and the brief encounters he had to endure when he ran into acquaintances while shopping.

His nervous energy was rather endearing, though, as he stood close to my mother and I, bracing himself for loose conversation and the whimsical "*Salut!*" from passersby.

Searching the crowd for my friends, I skimmed the windswept heads of fishermen bobbing with salt in their hair, waiting for the festivities to begin by scooping grime out from under their fingernails.

The front windows of the pub had been pushed completely open, and the doors were held taut with loose brick that had been kicked away from the building's foundation. Inside, the tables had been replaced with a horde of villagers, and Louie was vigorously pouring shots in tempo with fists banging on the bar in jubilation. More. More.

When a light waltz bridged to an abbreviated tango, the patrons around me fell in stride with the atmosphere. Swaying and singing and drinking, the close-knit merriment was wildly exciting. My head was swirling as my grandpa and I bounced on our heels, drinking beer and laughing at the men competing to win Louie's heart.

Grabbing my grandpa by the arm, I surfed through the frenzy. My mom intertwined with the old lady who sold Saint __ de Vie souvenirs just around the corner from the creamery. They danced together, chanting in unison, their necks weighed down by cheap plastic beads and threaded yarn.

Inside the pub, Louie saw me amongst the mass of tanned arms and surly men. Immediately standing atop the bar, he reached down to take my outstretched hand. With the ease that comes along with confidence and the burning warmth that comes along with vodka, I floated on shoulders and stepped across to the platform. Sweetly, Louie poured me a stein of beer. I whispered to him, pointing to my grandfather in the crowd.

Together, we ushered Papaly to the bar, enticing him with alcohol and obligation, to stand proud and drunkenly on top of it with us. Louie announced, with honor, that his oldest friend had decided to join us all for the festivities. After a firm handshake, a roaring cheer from the crowd, and a glorious pop of champagne, Papaly clinked his glass against Louie's and smiled with embarrassment.

Acknowledging that indiscretion had become the most prominent theme of the evening, I chugged my beer as politely as someone who despises beer could and looked out at the effusive flush of fishermen.

They jeered and jostled one another good-naturedly, the biggest spat between two cronies in the corner who each believed that their catch was the biggest of the day.

Glistening brown eyes caught my attention, and moments later they were calling out to me. Appoline, François, and Carlo all pushed through to the space below the bar, jumping and waving as they called my name. Six very flushed cheeks carried happily drunken smiles up to me.

"Jump!" the three of them yelled, waiting for me to come down, their fingers reaching for mine.

Once again caught up in the summertime novel of slow music and colorful butterflies that I was writing in my head, I turned around dramatically and stretched my arms wide open. Without bothering to look over my shoulder, I fell backward into the crowd, genuinely hoping someone would catch me, but content with the possibility that no one would.

Screams and laughter abounded above before I realized I had squeezed my eyes shut in fear.

"Je te donne, Bellamy!" Appoline shouted, her arms under my back.

"Je te donne, Bellamy!" François repeated, laughing heartily as he held the majority of my body up from crashing into the floor.

"Je te donne, Bellamy?" Carlo questioned from the spot behind, cradling my head with ease.

"You wouldn't get it, you weren't there," I joked, resting preciously in the arms of my friends.

The four of us laughed and shouted, and I allowed them to scold me for falling from the sky with no warning. Fortunately, I bought all of their forgiveness with a round of drinks and earnest kisses. It wasn't until we had a chugging contest that my toes began to tingle, and the stars above twisted their dust into a narration of my summer dream.

Nudging each other's sides, Appoline and I tried to distract the boys in any way we could, frothy Stella foaming at our mouths. Appoline and I won, finishing our beers before Carlo and François, both of whom claimed their glasses were filled with more.

"A ridiculous statement!" Appoline shouted.

"You can't be good at everything," I considered. "Stick to macarons."

François caught the snide remark and wrapped his arms around my neck playfully, while Carlo and Appoline argued over who could take more shots of whiskey.

"Mes amis." My friends, I cooed. "There's only one way to settle

this."

And with that definitive statement, we split a bottle of Louie's whole-whale special and bogged down under the peppered umbrellas that were sprinkled in disarray on the patio.

Thick, brown, syrupy liquid sat in stained shot glasses among the four of us. They shook, synced to the vibrations of the festival and shimmying to the stomps and gluttonous gulps that circled all about. In the distance, we heard clapping as a white-browed man was crowned with a beluga hat, my grandpa and Louie bestowing it upon him.

"I aspire to be him when I grow up," Carlo said in admiration. "One, by the way." He added this as he took a shot swiftly and nodded to Appoline, who matched him.

"Who? The man who's putting a whale on someone's head or the man wearing the whale on his head?" François asked, also taking a shot and eyeing me.

"Hey, watch it. That's my grandfather you're talking about," I chimed in, proudly setting down my empty shot glass.

"A Saint __ de Vie treasure, truly," Carlo assured me.

"Both of them." We all turned to Appoline as she spoke up. "I'd want to be the one giving the beluga crown and the one wearing it," she said.

"I think you're more of a salmon girl, if I do say so myself." Carlo adjusted his sunglasses, holding up his hands to her face as if framing her for a picture.

"I guess I'll take what I can get," Appoline laughed.

She took a second shot, signaling for the rest of us to follow her lead. Begrudgingly, we complied.

"Hey, it's not a race, it's a standoff," I implored.

"*Non, non.* See, my strategy is to rush into it quickly, to take you all out right away. Anyone can take ten shots in ten hours, but can you take ten shots in ten minutes?" Appoline winked at me, spiritedly competitive.

"So, your plan is to kill us, then?" I laughed.

"No, I'm assuming you'll all give up before taking the tenth shot."

We were in a stalemate.

"Ladies, please, calm down," François joked, placing his arm around my shoulder.

I sat across from Appoline, kicking her feet gently with mine. Carlo leaned in on the table, his face growing serious.

"If you think Carlo Castro, son of Carlo Castro, is going to surrender, then clearly you don't know me at all." He pounded his chest with his fist, ready for a showdown.

"Wait, you're a junior? Carlo Castro Junior? How did I not know that?" François chuckled, almost spilling the entire bottle of Louie's liquor across our laps.

"Shut up and drink. Three!" Carlo shouted, slamming his shot glass on the table, prepared for war.

We called the game Simon Does, as you didn't really get a say in whether you drank or not, unless you wanted to be declared the loser. Whenever a shot was taken by someone, the entire group had to follow, or risk another shot being taken before having enough time to catch up. If the group were to lap you, then it would be game over.

About five shots deep, we saw that the crowd had turned its attention and gathered around us. We picked up a few extra players; the timid girl I had seen in the pub my first night in Saint __ de Vie, a pair of ornery barbers, and an old woman who had originally only left her house to scold the party goers.

Thankfully, Carlo had sweet talked her into showing us all up, rather than shutting us down. Hunched closely together, it was hard to discern one browned arm or leg from another. Collapsed into a pile of sweaty bodies, we drank. I watched Appoline closely, waiting for a sign, yet nervous I wouldn't know what to do when I got one. Flirtatiously, Carlo pinched her waist when she drank, and François' hand grew comfortable against my lower back.

Drunk on this mystery liquor and perspiring with temptation, *La Fête des Baleines* proved to be an expressive and lively event.

"I'm so hungry," I whined.

"Well, there's a crêperie, oh you know, a block that way," Carlo said, alluding to the fact that if I were to leave, I'd be passed up in shots and forced to forfeit the game.

Something deep inside me stirred. With no hindsight or forethought given, I grabbed the bottle of maple liquor and poured myself a shot, draining it quickly. After relentlessly taking two more before the crowd, I stood with belligerent confidence and announced that I was going to get myself a crêpe.

"You have about ten minutes, I'd say, to take three shots. Have fun catching up. Pace yourself," I slurred, patting Carlo competitively on the back and waltzing toward Chez Suzette, where the crêpes were always warm and fresh. There was no way six people could take three shots before my return.

Behind me, I heard François and Appoline laughing and footsteps growing nearer.

"Bellamy!" Appoline brushed up against my side.

"You hungry? I'm getting a crêpe," I said.

We walked toward the storefront; the dusk settled on our shoulders.

"You're not as timid as you were when the summer started," she said, captivated and red-faced from the exuberance saturating the air.

"You're going to lose the game now, Appoline."

"Bah, I took the three shots, who do you think I am?" She banged on her chest the way Carlo had earlier, making fun of him.

"You think Appoline Alarie, daughter of Amélie Alarie, is a loser? *Bah non!*"

We giggled together in harmony.

"How much time do you think we have?" she asked.

"I give it twenty minutes," I said. "Old lady from down the block and François were both beginning to look green. We have time."

After ordering our ham and cheese crêpes, Appoline and I retreated to the alley by the side of the store, leaning against the exposed brick while I stuffed my face.

"Tiens," she said, nonchalantly handing me her crêpe as well.

"Why do you even bother ordering food anymore?" I chewed thoughtfully.

"Maybe one day, I'll surprise us all," she giggled, biting a piece off from the crêpe in my hand.

Concentrating on keeping both feet flat on the ground, I steadied myself through my core, imagining a rope stretching from my toes to my head.

"I wish I could go to New York," Appoline sighed.

"Hm?"

"Running around the city, away from everyone. Smoking cigarettes in the street, arguing with taxi drivers. It sounds…" She fumbled to find the right word.

"Smoggy?" I suggested.

"Bellamy. To be a bare face in a crowd. I'd give anything to be able to walk down the street in the pouring rain without *le curé* calling my parents to let them know he saw me with half a bottle of vodka in my hand."

"Maybe the issue isn't that *le curé* saw you with half a bottle of vodka in your hand. Maybe the issue is that you walk around midday drunk with half a bottle of vodka in your hand." I had finished my first crêpe and was genuinely saddened to see my left hand empty.

"Anonymous." The lightbulb in Appoline's head switched on quickly, as she ignored what I had just said. "Anonymity. New York would give me anonymity. I'd be anonymous."

"I didn't realize you were a celebrity here," I joked.

"Haven't you been paying attention?" she teased, going along with my remark. "I can't go anywhere without being noticed."

If I hadn't been so infused with alcohol, I probably wouldn't have kissed her in that moment as carelessly as I did. Pressed up against the decade-old brick, I consumed Appoline. The darkening time and ripened evening ushered me to a third act that I hadn't presumed was written yet. She kissed me back with hesitation, but I know it was only out of fear of being seen, because her ankles swarmed intimately around mine.

"Remind me to tell Louie to sell this stuff every year," I said as I pulled away, my right hand high above her head, holding onto her crêpe.

Appoline laughed brightly.

"*Oui*, I don't remember kissing anyone behind the crêperie at last year's festival."

"Oh, shit," my heart dropped.

"The festival!" Appoline and I guffawed, crashing our way back to La Baleine Bleue, where we found François dancing with the old woman who'd interrupted our game, and Carlo standing atop the picnic table, lecturing the crowd.

"Carlo?" we called to him. "What are you doing?"

"Oh, just let him be," François advised, hugging me cheerily from behind. "He took six shots, six fucking shots, while you were gone. He thinks that means he owns the pub now."

We all laughed as Carlo drunkenly listed off a slew of changes to his new pub. Sweetly, Appoline climbed atop the table with him and helped him down.

"Come on, *mon chéri*," she cooed. "You won. You get to wear the whale hat. You won the game."

"*Je suis la baleine!*" *I am the whale*, Carlo announced to us all, dragging his feet as Appoline supported his weight.

The crowd had petered out, and empty glasses of promise littered the venue, the result of another successful *Fête des Baleines*. The four of us; the calm and collected baker, the unruly hotel heiress, the wild son of Carlo Castro, and the visitor who found herself immersed in their lives, threaded our way uphill, toward the cottages overlooking it all.

"I wonder if your mom and grandfather made it back yet," François said, as we neared the stone-lined path of Papaly's lodge.

"I will genuinely be upset if I'm home before they are," I said, smiling and shaking my head.

"Carlo! That's not your house. Come on, it's this way!" Appoline shouted in the distance, rounding the side of the fence and jumping over it.

"*Au revoir, Bellamy! Bisous!*" Appoline blew kisses to me as she chased after Carlo, who was doing cartwheels to no avail, up the ascending slope.

I laughed. "*Bravo Carlo!*"

He hollered in thanks, and the pair of them raced off in skewed fashion, toward their respective realities of air and elegance uptown.

"*Attends!*" *Wait!* François shouted after them. "I'll come with!"

To this, Carlo turned around and stuck his tongue out at François. Appoline, amused, did the same.

"I think they'll be okay," I assured François, laughing as I stuck my tongue out back.

We stood at the hearth just outside the front door, looking keenly at one another.

"Thanks for walking me home," I said.

"Well, it was mostly to keep an eye on those two." François rolled his eyes and we traded smiles.

"For the record, if my hunger didn't get in the way, I would've won that game," I pointed out assuredly.

"For the record, you looked so sexy after you took those three shots, I would've liked to see you take three more."

François was really pushing his advances, seeing how far he could take it before I either gave in or ran away from the pressure.

"Goodnight, François," I blushed lightly, for once clean out of comebacks.

"*A bientôt, Bellamy.*" *See you soon*, he whispered, barely opening his lips as he did.

Standing strong and assertive, François grabbed my arm as I turned to open the door, inhaling when he brought my neck to his mouth. Lightly, he kissed me on one cheek, then the other.

"You almost forgot to kiss me goodbye." He bit his lip and began to walk away, but not before spinning around and sticking his tongue out at me from up the path.

I laughed heartily as the calm and collected baker waved, chipper and unaware of how my life played into the unruly hotel heiress's and the wild son of Carlo Castro's. François was only concerned with his and mine, in the very moment, nothing more. I think that was something I had always appreciated about him.

//

The days that followed Louie's festival would've been much harder to account for, had I not checked the calendar hanging in the kitchen religiously. The time spent at the beach and on picnics and canoeing recklessly was a blurry montage, a mix of watercolors running together aimlessly.

Summer on the seaside was beginning to fare well with me. In the early mornings, I'd take a walk with my grandfather to the bakery. We'd pick out three loaves of bread, one for me, one for him, and one for my mom, and stay to chat a little with François. He was growing used to seeing us at promptly an hour after sunrise, embellishing new creations and insisting flour on his face was just part of the baking magic.

Without ever truly making plans, somehow Appoline, Carlo, and I would end up together, causing harmless chaos while François worked his adult job. Though I would be returning to the States to work a job as well, I liked to pretend I was a boundless heiress with nothing but time, just like Appoline and Carlo. Alleviating the plateau of concern that the days would mold together out of paralleled consistency, we stayed focused in our attempt to find new activities each day.

One particular afternoon, Appoline and I were picking blackberries in a field just off the coast, a few miles down from Papaly's lodge. Aside from spotted embraces when everyone's backs were turned or eyes were closed, we hadn't circled back to our night at the hotel. Unspoken, yet quite tangible, it began to feel as though our lustful intentions had a poignant secrecy to them. Seeing as I wasn't sure what any of this meant, I wasn't bothered much by the risqué uncertainty of it all.

Tripping along the meadow, dewy with seaside mist, we waited for Carlo. He had assured us he'd be able to persuade his parents into letting him take their schooner out to sea, for educational purposes of course. Didn't we know? Carlo's goal was to, one day, captain great big commercial yachts. He had told us this in confidence on one of our late-night picnics, catered by François' day-old leftovers. I'm sure it was the champagne that told him to trust us with his secret ambition.

As we traipsed under moss-covered tree branches, I wondered if

Appoline and I would take things further than our coy entanglement of tongue and tongue, which seemed to be nothing more than a tease. Stopping in my tracks, I turned around to face Appoline, who had been trailing behind me. She had been chatting about possibly buying a puppy, but then she remembered she hated responsibility.

With sensual surreptitiousness, I held a blackberry in between my puckered lips. Grabbing Appoline by the waist, I drew her near, letting her take it from my mouth. As she chewed, I kissed her neck, my hands eager to run up her shirt, which blew so recklessly in the wind.

Alone, amongst only the forest and the secrets held discreetly in the gale, I capitalized on my desire. We rolled around on the grassy knoll, branches scratching our sides. Kissing, I removed her shirt, knowing we were safe from outliers and burden free, so long as time decided to pass us by while we lay atop dandelions, unseen by the world.

Gently, I slipped Appoline's bra strap off her shoulder, tempted to continue testing my limits. Kissing her collarbones, I reached around her back, unhooking her plain yellow bra, and casting it aside. We didn't speak as I licked in between her breasts, my legs inside hers, pinning her hips open.

Appoline was a delicate deity, hair splayed darkly in the grass, brown skin smooth and soft against my chest. Sunflowers and dandelions alike sprinkled their petals around her face, framing it so when I stopped to look down, I had no choice but to simply breathe her in.

"Do I look okay?" she asked, bashful for the first time, eyes hungry for acceptance. She had never been one to need reassurance.

I didn't answer, but instead bent my neck, kissing her breasts and finally tasting her nipples, shy and perky in the sun. Appoline squirmed with pleasure, only exciting me more, and I moved quickly to her hip, kissing and licking and biting.

Pushing her legs open, I sucked carefully on the inside of her thighs, my fingers running up and down her chest. Appoline moaned, and I could feel my indulgence heightening as I tried to ignore the anxiety in my hands, unsure what to do next. Pulling aggressively at her khaki shorts, I lifted myself up, slipping my arm down swiftly beneath, just over her underwear.

"Woah, Bellamy." Appoline's eyes opened, wide with surprise.

I lay on my side next to her, hand gentle, yet firm, in its place on the warmest part between her legs.

"We shouldn't," she said, clearly trying to convince herself.

I held her, cupped in my hand, feeling her heat.

"Don't you want me to kiss it?" I cooed, biting her ear.

Appoline sighed heavily, fighting herself, not wanting pure desire to take over.

"Come on." I kissed her neck lightly, grazing my fingers, tickling her mound. "Let me kiss you, I'll be gentle."

Buoyant and riding the waves of boldness, there was something quite calming about knowing Appoline was just as nervous as I was. Assuming she wouldn't let things go any further than they already had, I was confident in my approach and lustfully persistent. I knew I wouldn't have to worry about actually knowing what to do, because we would never get to that point.

The moment would end and we'd both be cordially regretful, yet secretly thankful that we didn't have to figure it all out in this one, embarrassing instant. Maybe the next one would do us better.

"We can't, Bellamy," Appoline said, just as I had expected.

She pushed me from her side and flipped over on her stomach, burying her head in her hands, elbows dug ashamedly in the ground. I sat up, crossing my legs, and pulling at the weeds in the grass.

"You keep denying me," I said.

"I want you," she mumbled.

"Until I start, then you want me to stop."

"I don't want to get hurt," Appoline conceded.

"I'm not going to hurt you. I thought we liked each other. I thought we were having fun." My fingers were tingling from the adrenaline of touching her.

"Not yet." She turned back over, lying her head in my lap.

Confused, I stroked her hair.

"My mother used to braid my hair for me every night before bed when I was little," I said.

"That must've been nice," she murmured.

"To have braided hair?"

"To have a mother who cared." Appoline reached up and pinched my chin with affection.

Before I could master a response to this, we were interrupted by a distant cawing of a strange, yet familiar melody. Hastily, Appoline threw on her shirt as we stood, accidentally crushing the pile of blackberries we had collected.

"*Un kilomètre à pied ça use, ça use...*" Carlo sang, emerging from the path just up the way.

"*Un kilomètre à pied ça use les souliers!*" Appoline and I sang back the children's nursery rhyme in response.

"You girls ready to set sail? The schooner is now Carlo's!" Carlo clapped, proud of himself and clearly excited to have made this announcement.

"You mean, Carlo Junior's?" I teased.

"Shut up, Bellamy! Weren't you two supposed to be picking blackberries? Looks like you rolled around in them instead. Women, so ridiculous. Can't do the simplest task," he huffed.

Appoline darted at him, jumping on his back.

"*Allons-y!*" *Let's go*, she shouted, and off we went, bumbling to the schooner that waited patiently for us, bobbing by the dock, asleep in the waves.

//

The day carried on impetuously, our inhibitions malleable to the vast wide open. François had met us at the marina, jumping onto the boat just moments before Carlo untied it and decided to venture off without him.

"Patience has never been your best quality, eh?" François sighed heavily, out of breath.

"What did you bring us?" I asked, grabbing the basket from François' hands, who then pushed Carlo playfully.

"A captain needs to make decisions in regard to what's best for his boat and his crew," Carlo said with ridiculous importance.

"For the hundredth time, we're not your crew," Appoline droned, rolling her eyes.

"Yeah, more like hostages," I said through a mouthful of warm brioche.

"May I remind you, none of you are wearing life jackets, and I reserve the right to push you overboard at any moment," Carlo replied with indignation.

"But then you wouldn't have anyone to show off to," François joked, and Carlo threw his hands in the air, surrendering.

"I give up." Carlo sighed. "Pass me *le jambon,* I'm hungry and these two already fucked up the blackberries."

Jovial misgivings and loose serendipity surrounded the tides that pushed us away from the chitter chatter of town. We had all grown accustomed to the constant dampness that came with living on the coast, so I stripped to my bathing suit in hopes that my insecurities would have the decency not to follow me out to sea.

Akin to a stomachache, or in this case, seasickness, I grew uneasy when Appoline mentioned my birthday. I had forgotten it was just a day away.

"With the way you put down liquor, I forget you're only twelve sometimes," Carlo teased, taking a sip of his beer in acknowledgment.

He was wearing a captain's hat he had pulled from the helm, and sat with ease, steering the boat lackadaisically.

"Twenty-one is hardly twelve," I said, legs up in the air, basking in the French sun.

"And red wine is hardly white, but they both get you equally as drunk," Carlo added.

"What the hell does that even mean, Junior?" Appoline laughed, sitting at the end of the table, tucked away with her farmer's hat flopping delicately over her face.

"It means that age is but a number," François reasoned, bare-chested and growing darker by the minute.

His blue swim trunks were plastered to his thighs, salty water leaving little to the imagination.

"You're disgusting. Twelve and twenty-one are very different. Pigs." Appoline muttered.

She was cradling a bottle of champagne, comfortable in her corner.

"*Oui*, but twenty-one and, say, thirty, are not. They are both adults." François said this as though Socrates himself couldn't have been more profound.

"Exactly my point, good sir!" Carlo drank in agreement, tipping his hat. "An adult is an adult, no matter the age, just like wine is wine, no matter the color. So, although you're the baby of the group, you're a baby that can consent."

"Literally, Carlo, the sea is getting to your head. You sound denser each time you speak." Appoline stood to steal the bread from François' lap.

"He has a point, Appoline," I stated smugly, flipping onto my stomach and stretching out. "No matter which way you look at it, I'm an adult. Just as much an adult as anyone else."

Knowing all eyes were upon me, I pulled at the string of my bikini top, untying it, and setting it beside me. Chest down, I let the stares of six brown eyes heat my back. They were still no match for the sun.

Somehow, Carlo returned us to shore safely, though entirely brined and pickled from the ocean water. Despite my friends' insistence on taking me uptown for a celebratory midnight drink, I declined, wiped from a week of light, yet perpetual movement.

Retreating to my grandfather's lodge, I saddled up for what I knew would be another passive birthday, holed away in my bedroom, somber and heavy. While my grandfather held no grudge, it hadn't grown any easier to look him in the eyes and ignore the weeping and heartache he had internalized for all these years.

We didn't talk about it. Never. I'm almost positive this is what made things even worse. My grandfather and mother both casting aside their pain, so as not to make me feel guilty, only made me feel even more guilty. Not only were they hurting, but they were hiding their hurt in an effort to protect me.

My birthday was always a guarded affair, a day of closed introspection. That is, until Appoline would come and sweep me away into the night, the first and final stop being the ice cream shop.

Chapter Sixteen

I SLEPT UNTIL NOON on my birthday, and after an egregious attempt at making my own espresso, I retreated back to the comfort of my darkened bedroom. Seeing as my grandfather and mother kept to themselves, only to ceremoniously sneak me money and weathered slices of black cherry gâteau Basque, I ventured out for a second and third time throughout the afternoon to experiment with the espresso machine.

By early evening, I had spoken to a total of three people if you included my own inner dialogue. When dusk rolled around and swept past my windows, I gathered my limbs and stepped outside to place some stones on the path, kissing them before dedicating them to my grandmother. I saw two stones that hadn't been there the day before. Clearly, my mother and grandfather had already paid their respects.

Shifting my attention back to the bay windows ajar in my bedroom, I waited in unease, hoping Appoline would show up just as she always had the many years before. We had yet to resolve the feelings that made it hard to swallow, so I wasn't sure if she was angry with me, or just indifferent.

At some point between darkness and night, I fell asleep, leaning on the edge of the windows, precious moments from falling to the ground below. I was awakened by a breezy pinch on the cheek. Appoline stood smiling, no grudge or doubt in sight.

"You're twenty-two today," she said smoothly, genuinely happy I was here for another year.

Appoline pulled me out of the window. Although I would never admit it, I had purposely fallen asleep in my favorite tank top and bleached jeans. I wanted to be pretty on my birthday.

"There's only one flavor of ice cream I haven't tried yet, you know," I said as Appoline and I held hands and ambled past the birdhouse swinging lightly overhead.

I avoided any talk of omens this time.

"Walnut," she stated. "I've gone with you to L'Écume de la Mer probably hundreds of times, and I've never seen you pick that one."

"Well, neither have you!" I reasoned, and we both laughed, the darkness a shawl around our shoulders.

When we circled the cul-de-sac, my excitement peaked. I nearly jumped over Appoline as I raced into the ice cream shop, as was tradition. Throwing the door open, I was genuinely surprised when the lights flickered to reveal the ice cream man was not alone behind the counter this year. In fact, standing beside him, giddy and flushed, was a long row of familiar Frenchmen.

"*Bon anniversaire!*" My mom, Papaly, François, Carlo, Louie, Saul, and even the old lady from the festival, all yelled in unison.

"Here." Appoline whispered.

She had snuck in before the door closed and handed me a giant bowl. I walked down the row of beaming faces, as each one scooped me their favorite flavor of frozen custard and added it to my bowl. Seven scoops for the seven years that I failed to return to Saint __de Vie. Confetti hung in the air like moss on oak trees, and I jumped with delight as François scooped me blueberry chunk and Papaly added sorbet. Beaming, I reveled in this gluttony.

When I got to Appoline, she eyed me happily, squinting between the walnut and the banana coconut. My eighth scoop.

"Surprise me," I whispered, closing my eyes.

Appoline dolloped a generous helping of banana coconut ice cream into my bowl.

"Next year, we can try the walnut. That way, you have to come back to me," she said, laughing piously.

"It's a deal," I winked.

The ice cream man then ceremoniously announced that all the *glace* would be on the house for the evening, as a gift to my many years of patronage. Seeing as I had never heard him speak before, I could have sworn his speech sounded a bit rehearsed, but maybe I was just being a tough critic. Come to find out, Appoline had helped him write down his whole speech on notecards the night before, so he wouldn't stutter in front of everyone. She also paid him a hefty sum in thanks for the free custard. Though she may have been wild and hard to pin down, she was always willing to give her time to the good people of Saint __ de Vie.

After giving the ice cream man a congenial hug and gentle kiss on the cheek, I thanked him for making the best frozen custard in town, and learned that he was named Maurice, after his grandfather. I told him I was named Bellamy Aramis, after my grandfather. This wasn't true in the least, and I'm not sure why I said it so suddenly, as if unable to control myself, but I'm glad I did. Maurice seemed quite delighted by the fact.

I never saw Maurice again after that night. When I came to visit Saint __ de Vie years later, I would learn that he had suffered from congenital heart failure and passed away in his sleep, with no one to leave his ice cream shop to. I would remember the moment that I told him my middle name was Aramis, and how he grinned so purely happy, unaware his ice cream shop would be converted into a magazine store once he was gone. And, while I'm ashamed to say it, I think it's important to note that the only ice cream sold there were freezer burnt chocolate drumsticks, packaged, and often disregarded. Frozen custard was not on the menu.

François came to steal me away from Maurice, embracing me with a gleam in his eyes I couldn't recognize.

"You're twenty-two today," he said, just as Appoline had earlier, except his tone was lustful and full of intent.

He told me I looked beautiful and made me promise to see him again before the end of the night, so he could give me my birthday present.

When Louie interrupted our conversation about what a whirlwind summer it had been, I shrieked out of simple adoration. He thanked me for getting my grandfather to come out to town again and gifted me a wrapped bottle of his worst liquor, an ode to the Festival of Whales. I kissed his cracked cheeks and bounded over to my mother and grandfather, who were sitting in serendipity on the bench across the shop, gnats swirling overhead in the streetlights and waiting for leftover custard.

"Maman! Papaly! Can you believe this?" I sat in between their arms, allowing them to cradle me like a child.

"*Oui*, Appoline had it planned since the first week we arrived, *ma chérie*." My mother pinched my cheek.

Paul Simon's voice blared from the store radio and my friends and family danced, probably unaware he was explaining that he'd rather be a sparrow than a snail. It was a gorgeous evening nonetheless, the ambience full of cake batter and merry villagers who were thankful for another reason to come together and celebrate nothing, yet everything, in this transient halo of time.

Papaly's laughter broke the seal of hazy peace that had glazed over my eyes.

"Quoi?" What? My mom asked him, savoring her butterscotch.

As he opened his mouth to explain, Papaly wheezed, choking on his own strawberry pie custard, in turn causing him to laugh some more.

"Are you okay?" I asked.

I patted his back, wondering where this mania had emerged from. Reddened and coughing, Papaly said it was quite curious that the day my grandmother died, she had been scolding me for eating too much on my birthday, and here we all were, indulging in frozen custard, feasting in her honor.

He continued to giggle, reminiscing and stating how angry at all of us she must be, looking down from above. My mom chuckled and crossed her arms, impersonating Mamaly. Both of them looked at me, grabbing the bowl and spoon out of my hand as a joke, reprimanding me for eating too much. They hollered in French laughter, cursive waves of sarcasm bordering the line of disrespecting the dead.

Astounded, I sat there until their laughing fit was over and Papaly carelessly handed me back my bowl of toppling custard.

"Mange ta glace. C'est la vie." He patted my knee and wandered off, giggling and shaking his head.

"Eat your damn ice cream," my mom repeated in English, scooting over on the bench. "It's life." She skipped off to spend the rest of the evening with Maurice, dancing on the cobbled roads and recalling her youth. I wouldn't learn this until after Maurice's death, but my mother had been schoolmates with him. She had known Maurice her entire life.

The cotton-draped tables and glass bottles of wine littered across the cul-de-sac were the first to tell of the rain. I was growing sleepy from the heavy cream and ripe plum juice settling in my stomach, so when I made a toast thanking all who had come to wish me a happy birthday, no one was surprised that I fell off the iron stool, tearing the side of my shirt.

More importantly, no one noticed that while I was picking myself up from the ground, Appoline was arguing with Carlo again, this time quite animatedly.

When Carlo lumbered away from Appoline and her shoulders melted with relief, I bumped against her side and wrapped my arms playfully around her neck.

"So, I heard you planned all of this?" I asked bashfully, wine sneaking up my throat and painting my face red.

"I mean, I had help from Maurice." Appoline smiled a tired smile.

She wasn't bubbly and wild, surfing the waves of existence, as she normally would.

"Are you okay? I was thinking, maybe we could sneak off to the hotel tonight." I walked my fingers down her spine, but she gently shied away from me.

"I can't tonight, Bellamy. I'm sorry."

"But, but it's my birthday. I didn't even get to spend time with you tonight..."

Appoline cut me off with her eyes, digging deeply into mine. Her stare hurt. I looked beyond her.

"Bell, I said I can't, okay? Just let things happen; stop trying to make them happen. It's life," she sighed, realizing how harsh she sounded. Her shoulders sagged, as though the rain that was now pouring over our faces weighed more than our burdens. "Hey, don't look so down. The entire village came out tonight to celebrate you."

Appoline pinched my cheek. Carlo, looking rather sullen, dragged his feet to our corner of the venue.

"You ready to go?" he asked Appoline, handing her his jacket.

She nodded and turned to me. "I'll take you to lunch tomorrow. Meet me uptown?"

"You're leaving?" I asked, embarrassed that the wine wasn't smooth enough to cover the cracks in my voice.

"Yeah, it's pouring rain and my mom needs me home. I'm sorry, Bellamy, but at least you got your ice cream." Appoline kissed me lightly on the cheek.

"Night, Bell. Happy birthday, and good luck on the toilet tomorrow." Carlo also kissed me goodbye, winking good-naturedly.

"The toilet?"

"*Oui*, you ate a lot, and I mean a lot of ice cream tonight. Be careful."

Had I not been so disappointed that they were leaving, I would have laughed at his joke. Appoline and Carlo ambled up toward the village's end and continued on until their figures were engulfed by the deepening night. The music was dwindling, and I watched with fondness as Louie and the old lady slow danced in the center of the iron tables, rain twinkling and matting down their hair.

Beside me, François came and handed me a glass of wine.

"Here, one last glass before I walk you home," he said, watching me as I watched them.

"Who put you in charge of walking me home?" I asked, engagingly defiant.

"No one, but I figured you'd enjoy the company. I promise I don't bite."

"You're doing that wrong." I nodded at his half-empty glass of blood-red wine.

François looked at me, confused. Holding my glass up to his, I tilted my head back and drained the entire thing in one effortless gulp.

"That's how you're supposed to do it." I smiled half-heartedly.

"I didn't realize it was such an art," he teased, and followed my lead, finishing his wine and setting his empty glass down next to mine.

They looked regal beside one another, shallow and clear. Taking one last look at Appoline and Carlo, I sighed and shrugged my shoulders.

"Oh, you're sad Appoline and Carlo left your party early? Come on, let them enjoy themselves." François winked, clearly unaware that his comments were not helping ease the sinking in my chest.

"How do you feel about carrying me home, instead? I drank so much wine, I don't think I can walk another step," I joked.

Almost instantly, and with ease, François scooped me up and threw me over his shoulder, sprinting away from the dimming streetlamps and rich smell of Maurice's sweet custard.

I laughed joyously, unarmed and free, my stomach aching in pain.

"What are you doing?" I shrieked.

"Carrying you home, don't tell me I'm doing this wrong, too?" he yelled in competition with the rushing air propelling past us.

We raced up the hill, my grandfather's cottage illuminated by lanterns in the ever-nearing distance. I hung off François' back, smelling the wind and letting it whip my hair around my face.

"Hey," I said as François slowed to a walk. "You said you had a present to give me."

François set me down and held my eyes in his. We stood in the middle of it all, where the village and the ocean and the cottages on the cliffs met, however I didn't feel as insignificant as I probably should have.

"I do, but it's at my house."

"Let's go there then. I don't want to go home anyway," I said.

"It's late."

"Good thing I'm a grown woman. I'm allowed to stay out late if I want," I smiled slyly.

"You're fun when you drink wine." François laughed.

"And when I don't drink wine?" I asked.

"Hey, no one can be perfect all the time," he joked.

I pushed him playfully and he grabbed my waist, forcing me to feel his desire.

"You know, you could've told me you wanted to go to my house before I carried you halfway back to yours," François pointed out.

"Well, clearly I have to make up for how boring I am when I'm sober."

We paused.

"I promised your grandfather you'd get home safely." François shook his head at me as we began our descent back into the village.

"You probably shouldn't make promises on other people's behalf," I reasoned.

When we arrived at François' quaint cottage, hidden calmly amongst the intricacies of town life, I ran inside, not allowing myself to think past my outstretched hand.

Sitting comfortably on his worn couch, I sunk into the memory, the experience of it all. Life would never catch up to where I was, yet no matter how hard I tried, I couldn't outrun its grasp.

After putting on a French record that I vaguely recognized, François opened a bottle of wine and set it before me on the coffee table.

"Glasses?" I asked, raising my eyebrows at him.

"*Non.* Tonight, we drink from the bottle."

"Time to let loose, huh?"

"I've been waiting for you to say that," he replied.

Leaning in, I grasped his thigh, the wine flirting infinitely with my fingers.

"Wait," François whispered delicately.

I didn't want to wait.

"Patience is not one of my virtues," I said.

François chuckled and retreated to the kitchen for a brief moment before returning with a large black cherry gâteau Basque, a beautiful ivory candle lit atop. In an angelic whisper, François wished me a happy birthday, careful not to accidentally blow out the candle himself.

With fruitful intuition, I blew out the candle, but didn't reach for a piece of the gâteau. I was saving my lips for something else.

"*Tiens.*" François handed me an opal box, tied simply with a lavender ribbon. When I opened it, I pulled out a white, collared shirt with blue stripes, just like the one I had gifted him in the beginning of summer.

"I want you to wear it tonight," François said smoothly.

In the unassuming dark with no candles left burning to light our faces, I stared directly into what I thought were François' eyes.

"Do you want me?" I asked bluntly, once again high on the boldness of wine and summertime magic that I believed was dictating the plot of my vacation.

My endless need to see my friends as characters in a story I was telling in my head definitely caused more damage than good, but I wouldn't realize this until much later. Real consequences had yet to emerge from my rash idealization of others.

"I've wanted you since the beginning," François replied. "You know that."

I was just a character in his story, the way he was in mine. This was another thing I appreciated about him. Detachment was bound to be a result of our relationship, but that was okay, because in this specific space in time, we were surging together.

"Okay," I said, succumbing to what I had been pushing away all summer.

My desire to be wanted had finally triumphed over who I wanted to desire me.

"You win," I whispered lightly in his ear, making sure my lips grazed his neck as I pulled away. "Show me how badly you want me," I demanded.

I couldn't see him, but I knew I wouldn't have to ask twice. For the second time that night, François scooped me up, this time with much more force than before. Just seconds passed before we tumbled into his bedroom. I could smell that his sheets had been freshly washed and a candle had been coincidentally lit. I blew it out. There was no need for light anymore.

"Tell me you want me," I breathed as François wasted no time in tearing off my favorite tank top.

"I want you," he huffed, as he threw me on his bed and rushed to unbutton my pants.

Had I been slightly less drunk than I was, I might have been turned off by this urgency. In the moment, his insistence translated to passion, and that was all I'd ever craved. Quite possibly, it was my greatest vice.

Lying on my back with just my bra and underwear on, I felt François grow more eager as I toyed playfully with his belt. Sturdy and unrelenting, he leaned down and kissed my neck, brushing my bra strap to the side.

"You're much tanner than you were the last time you were in my bed," he stated.

"It's been a long summer, François," I replied, the only words I'd say for the rest of the night. François undressed above me and helped me slip into a realm of what was, up until this moment, the swindling unknown, surreal yet definitive.

Everything happened so quickly, I wasn't sure if I enjoyed it or not. In fact, I actually had trouble remembering how it began and when it all ended. After a few grunts from François and a short burning sensation between my legs, I allowed the impulsive foolishness to consume my mind, which had grown fuzzy from the alcohol.

François was surprised when he saw the blood trickling down my leg, but he never ceased, adrenaline coursing through our veins like it, too, was drunk on wine.

I didn't cry when it was over, and I didn't feel much different when I saw the stain of dark blood on his wintry sheets. It was three in the morning when he finally rolled over and released his grasp from around my waist. I had been waiting wide awake for hours, as I despised being held while I was trying to fall sleep.

When I was positive that I had memorized the pattern of François' snores and was sure he was deeply asleep, I twisted out of his bed as silently as possible, wobbling from the uneasiness of the night, but mentally more conscious than I'd been before. I tiptoed out of his room, grabbing my clothes on the way.

Appoline's voice reminding me not to ever spend the night was on repeat, a phono in my ears. I passed the giant, uneaten black cherry gâteau Basque and blue pinstriped shirt, only taking a second to glance at it before realizing it was the exact shirt that I had given him. He had simply washed and folded it.

Rolling my eyes, I continued out the front door, leaving my gifts untouched. The only hint that I had ever been in François' house was the blood in his bed, the construct of purity forever undone on his freshly washed, white linen sheets.

Another birthday had come and gone. I was one year older, yet never the wiser. Crippling realization came over me once I stepped outside and began my ascent through town, back to the cottage. Walking through the barren cobbled streets of the village I had grown so fond of, I felt small. I wasn't regretful, at least not yet, but I was tiny, an unimportant part of a world that didn't know how to pause, even if it wanted to.

While I wandered past the bakery and the creamery, toward the dock, I sang happy birthday to myself. The boats bobbed as they always did, unaware everyone was asleep in their homes.

Well, I thought, I ate the damn ice cream, and now, for the first time in my life, I was finally full. Deciding I had all the time in the world, I sat on the edge of the wharf, my feet seducing the water just below. I pictured Appoline asleep with bottles of wine and an opened book at her side. She wasn't with me though. I was alone.

When I got home, it was nearly dawn. Quietly, I made my way to my bedroom, searching through my closet. For the first time since I had arrived in Saint __ de Vie, I pulled out Jean-Marc's sweater. Its bristles were itchy against my cheek, and although it no longer smelled of anyone in particular, I pretended it did.

I fell asleep in my closet that night. It was brief, but I slept, curled with Jean-Marc's sweater, the doors pulled almost completely shut by my feet. My final, lingering thought before I closed my eyes was that François was much more strategic than I had realized.

Chapter Seventeen

STARTLED BY THE SOUNDS of ambient life and creaking floorboards, I awoke, unsure where I was.

"Mom?" I murmured when I heard rustling on my bed from inside the closet.

Sitting up, I rubbed my head, my back hurting from the cold floor and awkward position I had scrunched myself into.

"We were supposed to meet uptown," Appoline's voice floated pleasantly from my bed.

"And yet, here you are," I grumbled, secretly delighted that she had snuck her way into my room.

Gathering myself and emerging shakily from the closet, I crawled on my knees, Jean-Marc's sweater over my raging mess of knotty hair.

"Looks like I've converted you," Appoline said, smugly nodding at the closet.

"It was the most uncomfortable few hours of my life, don't get a big head," I replied.

Climbing up off the floor, I sat awkwardly next to Appoline on the bed. I felt guilty for my conflict; desiring to devour her, while simultaneously unable to squash the memory of having slept with François just hours before. When the sweeping recollection of Appoline and Carlo's hasty departure from the party crept into my memory, I sat beside her much more at ease.

I had simply followed her lead. Had she not left with Carlo, I probably would have never left with François. My actions were her fault; that was the only way I could justify them.

"Sorry, about last night, Bell. For leaving so early." Appoline leaned her head on my shoulders.

I stiffened.

"Oh, don't worry about it, really. I can't believe you threw me a surprise party in the first place. You really outdid yourself," I replied mechanically. "I don't think I'll be eating custard again until next year."

"Shall we go grab lunch, then?" Appoline perked up immediately, never one to dwell too long on anything even remotely negative.

"Baby," I said, looking at her knowingly. "*Ma chérie,* does it look like I'm ready to grab lunch? I don't think I can even walk yet." I laughed.

"Aw, you're hungover. How adorable. It's always so precious when Americans try and drink with the French," Appoline teased, stroking my hair condescendingly.

"I am French." I rolled my eyes.

"Come on, I'll carry you if I have to." Appoline stood and bent her knees, waiting for me to hop on her back.

"How are you so hyper all the time?" I asked as it took all my might to topple heavily on her back from the bed.

"Weeeeee!" Appoline spun in circles, making us both dizzy.

Flashbacks of the night before, François running through the village while holding me on his back, swooped before my eyes. I shuddered. Appoline and I crashed onto my bed, out of breath and seizing from laughter, hers from delight, mine from agitation. Swirling in specks of mismanaged thoughts, I swam through my conscience, avoiding the icebergs in the way.

"Lunch?" I asked Appoline, her brush of hair silkily intertwined with mine.

"Lunch!" she repeated.

We left the cottage without saying goodbye to my mom or grandfather.

"I'll see them when I get back," I told Appoline.

In reality, I was afraid my mom might ask where I had spent the night, and I wasn't prepared to lie to her and Appoline. These kinds of deception take time and dedication to deliver and uphold. I couldn't commit to that.

After slipping through my bay window and out into the backyard, we capered gaily uptown. I wore a blue ribbon sewn into my braided hair, and Appoline threw pebbles high in the air, counting how long it took for them to fall to the ground.

"Where are we going to eat?" I asked when we were five minutes from the hotel.

"I don't know. I figured something would call to us." She shrugged happily.

The late summer morning was singing songs of renewal. The leaves weren't yet brown but were also no longer green. Change, or possibly evolution, was constantly being foreshadowed. Appoline asked me if I was excited to start my first job in the fall, and I told her my excitement came and went with time.

"When does it come?" she asked. I didn't have an answer. "Then why did you say it comes and goes?" Appoline was grilling me. I guess my excitement came when I found out I got the position but has been on the decline ever since, I tried to explain.

So, it doesn't come and go, Appoline stated. It came, and now it's dwindling. Sure, I could give her that.

"My excitement will come again when I get to New York, though," I decided. "Right now, it's out of sight. Out of sight, out of mind."

"That's a dangerous way to live your life," Appoline conceded.

For once, I felt firm in my stance.

"No one is one-hundred percent excited for something all the time," I countered.

"Well, maybe you should be pursuing the things that keep you excited," she replied.

I laughed, shaking my head at her. "There's no such thing," I said.

"Sure, there is!" Appoline threw a handful of tiny pebbles up into the air and pushed me out of the way before they all fell atop our heads.

"Name one thing that keeps you excited all the time," I demanded.

She contemplated for a moment, and I held back a haughty smile.

"See..." I muttered.

"Wine!" Appoline yelled in clarity.

We laughed and I rolled my eyes at her.

"You know what?" I said. "I agree with you. Liquor is the only thing I've ever seen you passionate about."

Though we chuckled and continued walking onto the smooth-paved roads of the elegance-situated uptown, I could tell Appoline was slightly offended. That's okay, I thought, she'll get over it. She always does.

Outside a quaint café covered in dark-blue umbrellas and stilted chairs, the pair of us waited to be seated. Appoline waved hello to a few passersby and exchanged kisses with a florist and her very slobbery dog. When we were seated and had ordered coffee, Appoline eyed me with a subtle, devious look.

"You know," she said, swirling a spoon in her coffee. "We've been alone for two hours and you haven't tried to kiss me. That must be a new record."

Before allowing my cheeks to glow with embarrassment, I

rebutted.

"I've decided to stop trying, considering you're constantly rejecting me," I teased.

"I don't reject you. I press you to wait for a more appropriate time. Pushing me up against the crêperie isn't exactly inconspicuous," she laughed.

"Okay, well then you let me know when it's an appropriate time for me to come on to you," I said.

She paused. "It's nice being up here every once in a while."

"Mmm," I sipped my coffee.

"No one knows me as well. It's almost like we're invisible."

She brushed her foot against mine underneath the table.

"Appoline, you said hello to five different people before we even sat down."

"*Oui*, but as we go farther away from the hotel, the people I know are less and less," she said.

"Are you trying to tell me something?" I asked.

The waiter came with our chocolate croissants. We smiled and thanked him before he recognized Appoline. In rapid French, they spoke. I rolled my eyes. Clearly, we weren't far away enough.

"Hey." An idea sparked in my mind when the waiter walked away.

"*Quoi?*" Appoline asked in her native tongue, still glowing and enchanted from her brief conversation.

I ignored this and continued. "Let's get out of here?"

"Can you let me eat my croissant first?" Appoline bugged her eyes out, annoyed.

"No, no, I mean. Let's get out of town. Let's go somewhere, for the weekend or something. Just you and I. Somewhere no one will know us."

This last sentence caught Appoline's attention, but she leaned in, still dubious.

"And how would we get there?" she asked.

"We can walk," I said with a straight face.

"I guess we could take the train," she mumbled to herself, ignoring me.

"Or run," I continued joking, but she didn't laugh.

"Maybe we can take my mom's old car. It just sits in the back garage." Appoline was contemplating with herself.

"I have twenty francs to contribute," I continued.

Appoline's face snapped up and she grabbed hold of my cheeks.

"Let's go. We'll do it. We'll take my mom's car. She doesn't use it." Appoline stood, in turn lifting me with her by the tight grasp she had on my face.

"You know how to drive?" I asked, perplexed and realizing I had never seen her drive.

"Kind of."

"What does kind of mean?"

"I know how to drive...but I'm technically not allowed to," she said slyly.

"And would you care to explain why that is?"

"It's nothing, really. Just happened to have a minor run-in with the statue of the mayor's grandfather in the center of town one night. The mayor might have taken away my license."

"Appoline!" I exclaimed. "Were you drunk?"

"Of course not! Just irresponsible," she said, shrugging this off.

"Then...how can you earn it back?"

"Ugh, the mayor wants me to make a public apology." Appoline waved her hand.

"And you haven't yet?"

"I will never apologize. I will walk the earth until I shrivel!" She banged her fist on the table in front of us.

"That's dramatic. It would be much easier to apologize. Probably better for your skin, too," I reasoned.

"Bellamy, are you in or are you out?"

We were both standing hunched over the small table, drawing confused stares from the other patrons as we devised our evil plan.

"Yeah," I said, looking around. "We definitely need to get out of here."

Squealing with glee, Appoline jumped and dashed past the café gate.

"Wait," I called, sprinting after her. "We need to pay!"

"Baby," she said, copying me from earlier this morning. "*Ma chérie*, does it look like I pay for my own food?"

I stared at her in casual disbelief.

"*Non,* I'm only kidding, but Martin paid for our meal," she said, shrugging.

"Who the hell is Martin?" I followed her away from the crowd of bumbling tourists.

"The waiter!" she exclaimed, and I couldn't help but laugh, my fondness of her growing with every 'I should have known better' moment.

Sneakily, we dashed behind the guesthouse of Appoline's manor, which sat just down the road from Hôtel Alarie. Why her parents needed a manor *and* a hotel was unclear to me, but I never bothered asking. Appoline rarely spent time at either, anyway.

A rack of keys hung in the shed, and we made a game of figuring out which one belonged to their yellow-painted Volkswagen. When we were successful, Appoline steered the car quietly down the street and parked, before running back to the house and leaving me waiting in rash anxiety.

"What was that about?" I asked when she returned and pulled away from the curb.

"Oh, I left a note for Muriel. Don't want her worrying," Appoline replied, smiling and taking my hand gently.

We drove along the coast, with the windows down and radio blaring, for about thirty minutes before I even bothered inquiring where we were headed.

"To my grandmother's!" Appoline shouted over the wind and music.

"Is she nice? My track record with grandmothers isn't the best!" I yelled back, hair whipping my face aggressively.

"She's dead!" she hollered, grinning broadly.

"What a relief!" I jested.

Our stomachs twirled in laughter, as I danced my hands out the windows to flutter in the wind.

"Oh, shit." I had a moment of realization.

"What? It's okay, really. She lived a long, happy life." Appoline turned down the music.

"No, no," I said carelessly. "Not that. I didn't tell my mom where I was going."

"There's a phone at my grandmother's. You can call her when we get there," Appoline reasoned.

As simple as that, Appoline and I continued our trip south, never leaving the coast, beachy water misting our hair. At various points during our drive, I lay in Appoline's lap with my feet out the window, steered the wheel while she manned the pedals, and slipped into the backseat to see what it would be like if she were my taxi driver.

"Two stars," I said, climbing back to the front seat.

"Two stars?" Appoline yelled incredulously.

"Appoline, you almost drove us off a cliff and offered me a

cigarette four times! I should be rating you one star, but since I like you, I'm being generous." I laughed.

She pinched my thigh. "I rate *you* two stars."

"You can't rate the passenger!" I exclaimed. "Only the driver gets rated!"

We kept on going, full speed ahead, never once looking back. If we didn't see it, it wasn't real.

When *"Je te donne,"* came on the radio, we screamed in unison.

"Perfect timing," Appoline said. "Bellamy, welcome to Saint-Jean-de-Luz."

Pulling onto a street that looked like it had been carved into the earth, I marveled at the lighthouses and tiny châteaux that sat defiant amongst the rugged waves of the crashing ocean. The town was a colloquial aggregation of medieval architecture, shops lifted above ground, making one feel as though life commenced at half speed down below.

We puttered around the village, not unlike Saint ___ de Vie, in the borrowed yellow Volkswagen, humming to the tune of the fishermen's bellows. I watched a seagull strip a toddler of her sun hat.

"Where's your grandmother's house?" I asked Appoline.

"There." She pointed up, away from the ocean, where a villa sat, sweating in the midsummer sun.

"That's not a house, Appoline."

Once again, I was in awe of the estate that gleamed in the distance.

"Non, but it will do," she winked.

//

Surprisingly enough, it only took a few minutes to reach the villa. The path leading from the village to the grandiose property started off craggy but evened out as we neared the sloping driveway. The lawns were green and watered, expanding at least two acres, a flat stretch of land settled amongst mountain and ocean.

The slatted roof was nestled cleanly atop a whitewashed manor with blue shutters and bronze crown molding.

"Woah, this is gorgeous," I said as Appoline parked the car on the gravel roundabout. "I shouldn't be on the lookout for a grandfather around here, should I?"

"No, he died before I was born. After my grandmother died last year, my parents wanted to sell this place, but I begged them to keep it. We vacation here sometimes on the weekends, but mostly, it stays empty," Appoline explained while we wandered toward the front door.

It was strange hearing her talk about her family in such a familiar way.

"Oh, I didn't realize your grandmother died so recently. I'm sorry, Appoline," I said, trying to gauge her mood by the way her head tilted to look up at the miniature castle before us.

"She adored this house," Appoline sighed. "Come on!"

She grabbed my hand and pushed open the oversized front door, revealing a grand and luxurious interior. Paintings of French royalty draped walls above pine floors, gleaming as if newly cleaned.

"I'm afraid to touch anything," I said, meandering through the great hall coated in white embroidered tapestries and unscented candlesticks.

"Why?" Appoline asked.

She had disappeared. I followed the sound of her voice into the kitchen, where she was sitting atop a gilded counter, sloppily eating from a jar of Nutella.

"Did you pull that from your shirt pocket, or...?" I let my inquiry trail off.

"No, I found it under that cupboard. I knew I'd left it here somewhere." She winked at me, gargling her response, mouth sticky with Nutella.

Appoline smiled, content. Take away everything and she would have been happy just to be alone here, sitting on the counter, eating the snacks she had stashed from her last stay. This was something I appreciated about her.

Simply and without reason, I gave her a gentle kiss on the cheek and continued roaming the house on my own, eager to remember this extravagance for future reference.

As years would pass by, I'd always revert back to my time at the villa on the hill in Saint-Jean-de-Luz. Only with time and its fading memory was it something that I found myself missing more, rather than less.

The terrace was my favorite spot on the property. Porcelain dishes and gold cutlery had been left spread out, as if a party had been prepared for but never engaged. I enjoyed sitting there on the balcony, overlooking the expanse of greenery and divots of ocean granite, imagining all my friends were there with me.

I was glad to be alone, though. It just happened to amuse me to dream of François and Carlo and Louie and Maurice and Appoline, with Spanish music playing as they all danced whimsically on the veranda.

We would eat foie gras and pour seltzer, indulging in the carelessness of it all, a life where champagne bottles never emptied, and the sun never set.

The idea of who my friends were, as narrated by the story in my head, consumed me. So again, I indulged in my lonesome envisioning and romanticizing of our existence, forgetting they had existed long before I had imagined them. Therein was my fatal flaw.

Wafting back inside, the ghosts of Saint ___ de Vie tiptoeing beside me, I stumbled upon an archway that led to what I presumed could only be a ballroom. The marble flooring was a bright contrast to its pine counterpart. It was here that I would spend my nights underneath the diamond chandelier, daring it to fall.

Appoline found me lying center stage, beneath the crystallized lights. I could smell the Nutella on her breath when she slipped above me, holding herself up with her arms, just inches away from my face.

"Brush your teeth," I joked, speaking before opening my eyes.

She kissed me.

"I thought you liked Nutella, though," Appoline whispered quietly when she pulled her lips away from mine.

"Yeah," I breathed. "It's my favorite."

Grabbing her waist, I drew her into me, body finally collapsing, no longer held strenuously overhead. Searching for answers in our embrace, I kissed her with the passion that came with knowing a thousand diamonds hung above us, their light sparkling in our hair. At least we had their blessing.

As I moved my mouth to Appoline's neck, she giggled and pressed my shoulders back down to the ground, forcing me to surrender. She moved eagerly to my sternum. Finally, I felt the reciprocation I had been longing for. Appoline teased me as her breasts rubbed my chest and her legs spread mine open. Before I was able to fully prepare myself for what I believed was to come next, she relented, dissolving into just another heavy body on mine. She kissed my cheek.

"I think we should go to the beach," Appoline stated with certainty.

"Why is that?" I asked, exasperated.

"You'll like it," she said. "Plus, I'm petrified that chandelier is going to fall on us."

Perky and understated, she rose. Things were much simpler here. I followed Appoline out of the house because I would have followed her anywhere. I was twenty-two and unafraid and feverish to take everything the world was offering me, no questions asked.

The sun plummeted, as if following us downhill. We parked on the edge of the coast and walked south down the sands, cars ambling by in the dusk. Appoline had bought me a black cherry gâteau Basque from a store three levels above ground.

"We're in the Basque country, home of the gâteau Basque!" she said when she realized exactly where she had driven us to.

A slight nudge of guilt trimmed my mind as I ate my treat, remembering the one François had made for my birthday. The only difference is that I actually ate Appoline's. In my mind, she drove hundreds of miles just to buy it for me.

I remember this night with such crisp clarity, it scares me to draw back on the memory. Appoline was cheeky and relaxed, comfortable again. She was playful, singing chipper thoughts of, "What if we just stayed here forever?"

She was no longer worn out and dreary, like she was at my party. I giggled in her excitement. She twirled me in circles and jumped on my back, kissing me with no hesitation or shame about her.

"It's nice to get away," Appoline said, sipping on the bottle of wine we had taken with us from the cellar at the villa.

The cellar was filled with red wines from ground to ceiling, so much so that I hadn't actually a clue what color the walls were. Appoline mentioned that her grandmother appreciated collecting red wines, and never had an empty spot on any of the racks that framed all four sides of the room.

"Do you ever drink them, then?" I asked.

"Of course," Appoline said, smiling as she took our evening choice of cabernet down from the shelf.

"We just always remember to fill the spot with a new bottle the next day."

I had made a mental note to stop by the grocery store in the morning. I pulled myself out of my reverie.

"Yeah," I agreed, my attention back to the beach, focusing on the moment before me. "It *is* nice to get away."

I gurgled, taking the bottle from Appoline and humoring myself with a generous swig. "No one to answer to."

"Exactly!" Appoline explained.

I chortled. "You don't answer to anyone anyway."

"Muriel runs a tight ship; I don't know what you're talking about," she insisted.

"Oh, shit. That reminds me, I need to call my mom and let her know where I am," I sighed.

"I thought we were free here!" Appoline exclaimed. "Bellamy Artois in Saint-Jean-de-Luz doesn't answer to anyone!" she yelled and jumped fearlessly into the night.

"Fuck it, I am free!" I shouted at the ocean, allowing its waves to drown out my drunken declaration.

"Besides," Appoline lowered her voice so the fish couldn't hear her. "Muriel probably told your mom you were with me, anyway."

"Thank goodness," I said, swallowing my relief. "I was starting to feel really bad. I knew it had been too long since Muriel had gossiped to anyone."

Our laughing carried us to a remote part of the beach, where the streetlights didn't reach. The only other people I could see weren't in the near vicinity. A couple was taking a moonlit walk in the opposite direction, and a group of friends looked to be having a bonfire a stretch away from us. No one bothered to give us a second glance. Being anonymous was quite liberating.

"You know something I've never done?" Appoline frowned at the wine bottle, now empty in the sand.

"Brought someone on a whim to your villa in the south of France for a romantic getaway?" was my cheeky response.

She waved her hand, "No, I do that all the time."

I pushed her playfully.

"What then?" I asked.

Appoline raised her eyebrows. "Gone skinny dipping."

"You know what, Appoline?" I laughed, lifting my shirt over my head, an instinctual response to her confession. "I am truly disappointed in you."

I threw my shirt on the ground and reached over, stripping Appoline's sweater off her body. She shrieked in compliance, clapping her hands. Quickly, we raced to unbutton our pants and tear off our socks.

"I like this Saint-Jean-de-Luz Appoline," I said, my arm around her waist as we attempted to run into the water, our bras and underwear the only thing left clinging to our shaky bodies.

We shrieked, the icy ocean nipping at our toes.

"I like Saint-Jean-de-Luz Appoline, too," she laughed, unbuttoning her bra and throwing it behind us.

I discarded my underwear, looking ahead and refusing to even glance at Appoline. Naked and unassuming, we stormed the sea, prepared to take on all that we weren't ready for. The water was so cold, I never even saw Appoline bare. The blackened ocean clothed us.

"How are we doing this?" I yelled over the tide, jumping with the current.

"I have no idea!" Appoline shouted back to me.

"We should be cold, right?"

"Maybe we're invincible!" Appoline surmised.

"I think we're just drunk!" I decided, splashing in the ocean, one wrong gust of tidal waves from floating away forever.

We returned to shore, running far from whatever was chasing us. I left it all behind and crucified myself for allowing any of it to just be a story. I should have given more, but that's the thing about regrets: we don't have them until it's too late.

"Do you believe in soulmates?" Appoline asked me when we had dressed, our clothes sopping wet, seaweed caught in my hair, sand on her face.

We clung together for warmth.

"No," I answered. "There's too many people on Earth to rely on just one."

Appoline contemplated.

"What about you? Do you believe in soulmates?" I asked her.

"Of course," she said straight away. "What would be the point in living without them?"

"What if you never find them, though?" I squeezed the water out of my hair as we continued walking down the shore.

"I think I'd be happy just knowing they're out there somewhere. Knowing they were looking for me, too," she replied.

We stumbled across a nook in the ocean where large mossy rocks staged a fight with the waves, brawling for territorial rights. I could have sworn I heard an argument brewing amongst the elements, but wrote it off as the sounds of a chatty midnight sea.

Shivering, I hopped from rock to rock. When I found one large enough, protruding from the highest crash of water, I grabbed Appoline. We stood atop the rock in the spray, staring out into the ocean. We were endless. I kissed her deeply, hoping she'd remember this moment forever, hoping she'd never forget me. I was selfish and delighted, wanting her to want me more than anything else she'd ever wanted.

Cheeks peachy and eyelashes frozen with sea mist, Appoline and I scurried carelessly down the shore, where a group of men were gathered, night fishing. They were singing in Spanish and shouting at one another with vivacity. Lanterns were hung romantically on their docked boat, large towels and woven baskets splayed on the seafront.

As we passed by, one of them called to us in French. I didn't quite hear what he said.

"Sorry?" I shouted lightly back, forgetting I was speaking English.

Appoline and I ambled a little closer to the group. The one who had called out to us smiled, excited.

"Oh, you are Americans?" he asked.

"Sure, we can be," Appoline decided, friendly and nonchalant, bumping my side with her hip.

We were facing the man, who was wearing a simple t-shirt and jeans, his arms weathered and stretched, muscles twitching with every movement he made.

"Do you *señoritas* want to see some sharks?" He raised his eyebrows.

"Oh, very funny," I laughed uneasily.

I turned to continue walking, when Appoline grabbed my hand. Behind us, another Spanish man was standing, holding up a three-foot-long baby shark by the tail. We screamed.

"Oh, shit. I didn't realize you were serious." I exhausted the pounding in my chest.

"That's a shark?" Appoline squealed in disbelief.

"*Sí*. We're fishermen, we're nothing but serious when it comes to our catch," the first man said.

"What are you going to do with them?" I asked, squinting at the others as I saw them corralling more baby sharks into the woven baskets.

The sharks squirmed and flopped, a useless attempt at freedom. At least they weren't alone. The fishermen must have caught an entire family.

"We make ceviche with them," our new friend told us, smiling with such proud innocence. "The best in town. That's why we don't share with anyone."

In Spanish, the other men motioned with their arms and told us to come closer. They were hauling the giant sea creatures from the boat to the ground, working together in the lantern light, guided by their leader, the moon.

"Do you want to cut one open?" the man asked us.

"What? You do it right here?" I shuddered.

"Of course. It's so fresh."

"No, I'm okay..." I began to say, but Appoline cut me off, jumping in with zeal.

"I'll do it!"

She was antsy and keen, her face lit up from a cocktail of wine, wind, and excitement.

"*Muy bien!*" The fisherman, whose name I never learned, clapped his hands in surety.

He tossed Appoline a carving knife, as two other fishermen laid one of the sharks in front of us on the tarp.

That night in Saint-Jean-de-Luz, with shark's blood splattered down her arms and dotting her cheeks, I knew I would be running from the way her laugh made me feel for the rest of my life. I tiptoed, skipped, jumped, and paced methodically on the edge of the cliff, while Appoline made friends with the fishermen.

I couldn't stand still, so I danced with the wind. Appoline almost fell. She was so enamored with the dying baby sharks hanging upside down in front of our faces, that she lost footing. They squirmed. We watched, enthralled, as they fought with the air, as they fought with gravity. I watched as they fought with life, as they fought with Appoline.

Fuck, I remember thinking. *We are so screwed.* We both knew it, too. Uncanny danger lingered in the water and slipped over her fingers. The baby shark was so helpless. It begged to be freed from Appoline's grasp as she plunged the knife through its belly and dragged it savagely through its fickle flesh.

She carved the Mona Lisa smile on its underside. Bloodied and raw, I was exuberant despite the loss of life around me. The devil was sad, and so were the baby sharks. But us, we were so happy.

Appoline looked at all of us for reassurance, her eyes glowing as all the Spanish fishermen applauded her. She was a natural! I shook my head in disbelief.

After saying farewell to the Spaniards and insisting we couldn't stay any longer, we gave our friend a kiss. They all assured us that they fished in that exact spot, every weekend. *Come back anytime,* our friend said. He threw Appoline a towel to wipe off the blood she had acquired.

"Keep it." He winked and turned back to his group.

"I cannot believe you did that," I stuttered as we walked away.

"It was going to die, either way," Appoline reasoned with me.

The haul back to the car felt a lot longer than the descent down the shore. It was well past one in the morning when we returned to the villa on the hill, and although my body was tired, I was craving a comfort I couldn't quite put my finger on.

//

"This was my room." Appoline opened the door to an immaculate bedroom on the third floor. Threes had not ceased to follow me since the start of my vacation.

"Is," I corrected her. "It *is* your room."

The Victorian-styled bedroom had dark drapes and quilted furniture. There was a small sitting room off to the right of the bathroom, and a glass door at the foot of the bed opened up to a miniature balcony. Large oval frames, encompassing portraits of people whose visages I could recall but couldn't name, hung on opposite ends of the walls.

Appoline's king-sized bed was shrouded beneath a canopy of blossoming blue and lavender. I slid my shoes off, then slowly undressed before slipping into the cotton sheets. The lights were off, because we had never turned them on, and I felt Appoline crawl in beside me.

"You know what the fisherman told me while I was cutting open that shark?" she whispered.

"Nice boobs?" I whispered back, half-joking, half-asleep, and half-drunk.

Appoline smirked. I couldn't see it, but I know she did.

"He said that tourists always come here thinking that the *luz*, in Saint-Jean-de-Luz, means light. Like la Côte de Lumière."

"It doesn't?"

"Nope. It translates to muddy place or something. How about that?" She seemed proud of herself for sharing this newfound knowledge with me.

"Sounds like they should just continue to let tourists think the former." I yawned.

"It's crazy, I've been coming here since I was a child and never knew that. I always thought I was traveling from one place of light to the next." She nuzzled closely to me on her side. "This whole time it's just been mud."

The balcony door was propped open, allowing a nosy sea breeze to travel through the room.

"I'm chilly," I said. "Do you have a sweater I can borrow?"

"Yeah, in the closet over there." Appoline nodded toward a double-doored closet.

Wrapping the duvet around me, so as not to walk as Eve did before the garden was filled with shame, I trudged across the room. Upon opening the doors to the marvelously grand walk-in closet, I saw something that shouldn't have surprised me. A makeshift bed was constructed delicately on the closet floor. Two pillows, fluffy and much too lavish to be on the ground, laid atop a linen sheet and scatter of sweaters.

"Oh, Appoline," I sighed. "You really have an aversion to beds, huh?"

Appoline sat up quickly, embarrassed.

"It's nothing. Grab a sweater and come back to me."

I couldn't refuse that offer, so I threw on the first thing I could find and hopped back into bed, pulling Appoline close.

"It is rather chilly," she agreed.

Laughing, I stretched the woolen sweater over her head, and we guffawed as she poked her neck through the hole where my head was. In doing so, our bodies came together. This was when I realized, Appoline was naked, too.

Her skin was soft, and though I expected it, her softness still made my legs tremble. Our thighs overlapped and she hugged me, chest to chest, knees knobby and awkward, hitting one another.

"Wow, the sweater is a perfect fit," I mumbled in her ear.

She laughed loudly.

"My grandmother was a large woman. This one was hers," Appoline explained as we held each other tightly, wrapped in the sweater as one.

"I like it here," I said, my hands wandering down her bare back to her legs.

I grabbed her thigh and threw her hips over mine. I wanted her to envelop me.

"Aren't you going to kiss me?" Appoline asked, wide eyed and resolute.

This surprised me, considering I had always been the one to ask such questions. I had been the one to roll my eyes and swallow my pride. If I hadn't been so blunt from the beginning, we may have never kissed in the first place. She knew this, of course.

Unfortunately, as much as I wanted to kiss her lips and swallow her taste of almonds and honey, I couldn't quash my guilt. It kept creeping up on me, like the way spring creeps upon winter. I ducked my head out from the sweater and worked my way down her body, licking her stomach.

"What are you doing?" she mumbled.

"Kissing you," I said, biting her thigh.

She moaned, and it was enough to convince me to keep going. François wasn't going to dictate this night. My mouth finally stumbled upon the warmest part between her legs. She smelled like a woman. I kissed gently, without opening her up. She was smooth and tender, her legs tense but inviting.

Before I could continue, Appoline sat up, throwing the sweater angrily across the room. I froze, afraid I had done something wrong. Thank goodness wine had powered our evening, otherwise I would have never had the courage to even make it as far as I had.

"Lie down," she said.

"What?" Confusion toppled over me.

"Lie down. I want you. I want you, first," Appoline whispered, grasping my throat and firmly pushing me down on the bed, discarded sheets and pillows all around us.

"You want me?" I stammered, out of breath.

"Of course I want you, Bellamy. You're all I think about."

Appoline began licking me from right below my bellybutton, all the way up to my mouth. With her hands, she lifted my hips into the air, kissing my neck and spreading my legs open with hers. We were entangled.

She was beautiful to look at, in between my thighs. I took comfort in realizing that I was present for this moment, but as she engulfed all that I had to offer, I hesitated. She felt a pause in my breathing and looked up at me.

"What?" Her eyebrows furrowed with concern. "Are you okay?"

"I slept with François last night," I admitted, rushing to get it out of my mouth and over with.

Appoline's face went slack, and I watched as her eyes numbed. I did this to her. Slowly, she knelt and gathered a pleated pillow in front of her naked body. I pulled the covers up to my shoulders.

"Why?" she managed to ask, her nostrils flaring with an abridged sadness I had not seen until this point.

"I...I don't know. He wanted me," I shrugged, my voice wavering.

"But I want you," Appoline replied, dumbfounded.

"He wanted me when you didn't," I answered, shaky and beginning to sweat.

"I've wanted you this whole time. What are you talking about?" Appoline was appalled.

"No, Appoline. You went home with Carlo last night. I know you slept with him. I was drunk and sad, and François was there, wanting me."

"Wow," she said quietly. "You really don't know anything."

"I take offense to that," I said, growing nervous.

"I take offense to you sleeping with François last night and then having the audacity to let me..." Her voice softened. "Go where he was."

She was embarrassed and bashful, her face bright, yet hurt. Her black hair framed her cheeks with innocence. I swallowed, feeling guiltier than ever.

"He—he wasn't there like you were," I mustered.

"That doesn't make it any better, Bellamy!" she yelled, taking us both by surprise. "You slept with him because he made you feel wanted when I didn't? So was he the second choice, or am I?" she continued.

I hung my head, unable to look at her.

"I feel stupid. I thought we were something." Appoline's voice shook.

"Well, I had no idea what we were." I was growing angry. "You wouldn't talk about it with me. And every time I did anything, you pushed me off like you were ashamed. How was I supposed to know how you felt if you denied it every chance you got?"

"I wasn't denying you! Saint __ de Vie is a conservative town, Bellamy." She sounded defeated.

"Who fucking cares?" I shouted. "You just don't know what you want with me."

"Who fucking cares?" she yelled back at me. "I fucking care, because *I* live there. *I* know everyone in town. *I* have my parents' business and reputation to uphold. The only reason you don't care is because you get to run away at the end of the summer, before any gossip would ever reach your family."

"It's not running away. Sorry I have a career to pursue and actual goals I want to accomplish. I'm trying to make something of myself," I shot back at her.

Appoline retracted in underscored hurt. I was always taking things a step too far.

"I'm going to run that hotel one day, Bellamy. Don't tell me I won't make anything of myself." She stretched her neck in indignance.

"That's not what you want to make of yourself, though," I countered.

"It's none of your business what I make of myself," she said.

"Then it's none of your business who I sleep with," I decided.

"Fine. That's all you wanted, anyway." Appoline grabbed her clothes off the floor and thrust them on quickly.

"What's that supposed to mean?" I rolled my eyes.

"François, me. It doesn't matter who it is, you just wanted to get laid. That's clear now," she said.

"You know that's not true." I lowered my voice. "I've been after you all summer. I just felt like I was chasing a dead end. And you know what? I don't know why you're persecuting me when you're the one who left with Carlo in the first place. I asked you to stay! I wanted to go home with you! But you chose him!"

Appoline huffed with disdain and shook her head.

"Do you know why I left with him? Because my dad was back in town, and I pretend I'm dating Carlo in front of him, for appearances. My mom makes me, so he won't disown me."

"Is Carlo Prince fucking Charming? Why would your father disown you for not dating him?"

At this point, I was livid. Not only was Appoline hiding her secret, fake boyfriend from me, but she was now dressed while I was still naked. The power dynamic had definitely shifted.

"UGH!" She let out a frustrated scream. "Because they caught me with a girl! And now, if I don't pretend that I have a boyfriend and right my wrong, he's going to disown me."

I felt a wash of cold truth slap me in the face. I was stunned. Appoline kicked the pillow on the floor.

"There's another girl?" I asked.

Though in retrospect, I knew it was unfair; I was jealous. I thought I was the only girl Appoline wanted.

"Was," she sighed. "There was another girl."

I softened. "Are you going to explain, or are you going to make me beg?"

Appoline paced back and forth, aggravated steps making the floorboards grumble.

"It was nothing. Just a girl I met a year ago. She was an au pair for a wealthy family in town, staying for six months on exchange from England."

My stomach grew uneasy. I thought I knew Appoline, yet now I wasn't even sure I knew myself.

"We, we, I don't know. I don't understand it. I liked her a lot. One day, the parents she nannied for came home and saw us, together. It would have been fine, but they're regulars at the hotel restaurant, and they told my mom and dad about it. I wasn't allowed to see her anymore, and she left to go back home without even saying goodbye." Appoline looked at me before continuing.

"I thought it was a fluke. Maybe I was confused about our friendship. I don't know. All I know is that my dad was furious. He threatened to kick me out. The only reason he didn't is because Muriel and my mom wouldn't let him. He's gone away on trips so often that it doesn't make a difference." She scratched her scalp anxiously. I practiced my breathing.

"He's still angry, so my mom makes me bring Carlo by every now and then, especially when I attend parties or events. Carlo hates it. Feels like I'm using him. But this whole thing has really caused problems between my parents. My mom thinks my dad will lighten up if he realizes I've changed and have a boyfriend. I must've just been *mistaken*." She hung her head.

I remembered back to the day when I was doing cartwheels on the cliff up shore. I had seen Appoline's mom and dad emerge from the courthouse, disgruntled. Now, it made sense.

"Appoline, I had no idea. Why wouldn't you tell me any of this?" I asked her.

"Why would I? When you showed up, I was bouncing from guy to guy, trying so hard to find what I had lost. I wanted to feel what I'd felt with her. I didn't think it was possible, until you came around looking at me with your stupid green eyes." Appoline chuckled lightly, angry at the world.

"Don't you think this would have been helpful information for me to know?" I asked, still annoyed I had been left in the dark for so long.

"No. It had nothing to do with you, or us."

I gave her a knowing look.

"I wanted to keep you in a box, for myself. I didn't want to say too much and ruin things," she said.

"Well, you didn't say enough," I replied.

"It doesn't matter," Appoline sighed. "You're going to leave in a week anyway. None of it matters. You'll leave just like she did."

"You can't seriously be blaming me for being an American? You're mad because I'm going back to America to start my job?" I scoffed.

"No, I'm mad you can't stay. I'm mad that I tried so hard to keep you at a distance, all for you to reel me in and make me feel safe. But it's a false sense of security, because you're going to leave and we'll be continents apart. I'm not stupid. I may be an optimist, but I'm not insane. All we'll ever have is this summer, these moments. That's why I didn't want to sleep with you. I didn't want to have the memory of what I was missing replaying over and over and over again in my head once you've gone." Appoline was out of breath, her eyes welling with beautiful tears that I hated to see.

"I'm sorry." I swallowed. "Come on, we don't have to do anything. Just come sleep with me, please? It's late. We don't have to keep talking about this, just come to bed."

I took her hand and brought her back to the canopied bed, trying to stabilize my shakiness. While I was exhausted, afraid the sun would come up before we'd close our eyes, I was also barraged by uncertainty. My emotions were unclear, and there was no way I could decipher them with Appoline looking at me through her broken soul.

She lay on her side and let me cuddle her. I held her tight, sleepy from the extent of our argument. The wine was creeping up my spine, into my neck.

"Fuck François," she whispered.

"Fuck François," I agreed, mostly for her benefit.

"Fuck him. He's thirty-six. He has no right sleeping with you." Appoline held my hand in hers.

"Yeah, we don't have to talk about it," I said.

I kissed her forehead, and slowly let the exhaustion of anger take control and put me to sleep while I held Appoline. Again, this was for her benefit, not mine.

It felt as though I had been asleep for just a few minutes. I awoke, no longer cradling the girl I had lusted for all summer. I turned over, afraid she had left me.

"Appoline?" I called, sitting up.

There was no response. Quickly, I stood, searching for my clothes in the dark, when I remembered to check the closet. As quiet as possible, I opened the closet door and found Appoline snuggled beneath a sheet, her head soft against the pillow on the ground. Sighing with relief, I knelt down, squeezing into the space beside her. She looked so innocent; a precious girl asleep in her closet.

"Hey." I kissed her cheek. "I'm here."

Appoline grumbled, opening her eyes just a sliver.

"You don't have to sleep in here with me. I know it's not ideal," Appoline said.

I laughed good-heartedly. "No, it's definitely not ideal, but I don't mind. I want to be with you."

"Okay. Then shut the door," she said. "It needs to be pitch black in here."

I pulled the doors shut and let the weight of nothing surround us. Appoline turned on her side. I scooped her in my arms, my hand reaching beneath the pillow. I felt something beaded slip across my fingers. Tugging lightly, I pulled the beads out from under the pillow.

"Appoline," I whispered. "Is this a rosary?"

Appoline stiffened in my arms. Her breathing increased.

"Yeah," she exhaled.

"Why is there a rosary in your closet? What's it doing under your pillow?" I asked.

She didn't answer. I let the beads slip through my thumb and forefinger, remembering we were both Catholic. Visions of walking to the altar and taking communion glowed in my memory. The pair of us grew up attending the church on the cliff in Saint __ de Vie. I wondered what had happened to that.

"My grandmother would put it there," she explained. "On the bad nights."

I didn't say anything, just squeezed her close to me.

"When I first got caught with that girl, I would come here to get away from everyone and everything. My parents were constantly fighting. My dad hated me. My mom begged me to change. I didn't know what to do, so I'd stay with my grandmother here. She was alone in this big house, anyway."

"That makes sense." I said, proceeding with caution. "Is that when you started drinking?"

I wanted Appoline to feel safe enough to confide in me.

"I've been drinking since I was ten, but yeah, my grandmother does have a charming wine cellar," she conceded. "Nighttime was always the worst. I'd toss and turn in bed. No matter what I did, it was always too bright in my room. I couldn't sleep with myself, my sins showcased in the light. There was always too much space. I felt like I'd be swallowed whole by guilt and shame. So one night, I came into my closet. At first, it was to pray, to beg God to absolve me, but I had no words. I lay down instead. It was the first time I had gotten a full night's sleep. In the morning, when I didn't come down for breakfast, my grandmother found me in here. After that, she'd come and check on me every night, and like clockwork, every night, she'd find me in the closet, shaking with just this impenetrable anxiety. I remember the night she put that rosary under my pillow. I'm not sure she had any clue what was going on. Maybe she knew it all. I really don't know. She was scared I wasn't going to make it, but she came into the closet and knelt down and told me I could always talk to God, no matter where I was sleeping, or how."

Appoline was fragile, and my eyes burned. I tried desperately to stay strong for her.

"Or with whom," I added.

"She didn't say that," Appoline sniffled.

"No, but we can pretend she did." My voice shook, dying out at the end of every word.

"Maybe," she said, not convinced.

"Why do you like it in here?" I asked.

"I like not ever knowing if my eyes are open or not, because it's too dark to tell. It's peaceful. There's too much to deal with out there, in bed. Maybe I don't deserve it. I get as close to happy as I'll ever be, while I'm in here, eyes open with nothing to see," she whispered.

"Do you ever think you'll be happy?" I asked, my heart breaking for the pain she was feeling.

"I don't think I'll ever get sick of sleeping in the closet," she answered.

We fell asleep, close together, the doors to the closet shut, my head next to hers. I had one hand on Appoline's shoulder, the other wrapped so tightly around the rosary I awoke with the imprint of marbled beads on my fingertips, a cross embossed on my palm.

Chapter Eighteen

WE DIDN'T REALIZE IT was the next morning until it was actually afternoon. The closet had done its job and shielded all light from disturbing our slumber.

By the time Appoline and I had both showered, dressed, and made ourselves a reparative cup of tea, it was already the part of day where the sun shone the brightest, a prequel to its matinée show of setting. Neither of us had mentioned the previous night. Instead, we engaged in all the simple things that one might do to stay busy.

At the grocery store, we bought three bottles of red wine, one to fill the space from which we took a bottle the evening before, and the other two for each of us to drink with dinner. We also bought ourselves two baguettes and the ingredients to make half of a lot of dishes, but a whole of none.

As we boiled vegetables and sipped on red wine, we spoke of arbitrary ideas, avoiding what was important. We were pretending, and while we put in all our effort at doing so, neither of us were good at acting. Together, we sat on the terrace, deciding the best solution to our problem was to get blindingly drunk.

"Imagine a world where nobody cared," Appoline said after her fourth glass of wine. "About anything."

"That's the world I try to live in, every single day," I said.

We laughed, intoxicated. There was nothing pushing the plot of our plan forward, so we carelessly indulged in what we had before us.

"I wish I could go to New York with you," Appoline admitted once again.

"We could get a house together," I offered.

"Where? In France or New York?" she asked.

"Somewhere in the middle, maybe?"

"Oh good, I've always heard the Atlantic was a nice place to start a family," Appoline joked, raising her glass at me.

I spit out my drink, laughing much too hard at such a simple statement.

"Hey, I have a question for you," I said, after we pretended to enjoy the silence of watching the birds fly over us.

"Lay it on me." Appoline had her eyes closed and her feet up on the glass table.

"Why did you push me so hard to date François?" I asked.

Appoline kept her eyes shut.

"I don't know. I think I was testing you. I was probably testing François, and I was definitely testing myself. I wanted to see if you'd go for it. I had this crazy notion that you were into me, but I couldn't tell, so I urged you to date him, hoping you would, and I could move on," Appoline explained.

"You wanted me to like François?" I begged her to clarify.

"At this point, I definitely think it would have made things a lot easier," she laughed.

"What are we going to do?" I asked her.

"I don't think I'll ever know the answer to that question," she responded. "But hey, thank you for being my Emily, for wandering here with me."

I turned to look at Appoline, the sun setting on her face. I knew she was remembering the night we first kissed, when she asked me to be her Emily, just so I'd go into town and let her buy me frozen custard. I remembered it, too.

"Busted. You found me," I said lightly. "I'll always be your Emily."

She smiled softly and nodded her head. We were sitting two chairs apart, afraid to touch and accidentally remind ourselves that there would be a last time for it all, and that time was soon.

"That reminds me." I jumped up, grabbed the stereo from inside the house, and returned.

I held up a Paul Simon and Art Garfunkel CD.

"What's that?" She squinted.

"I bought it at the record store next to the boulangerie," I said. "It's my going away gift to you. Since we've been listening to them sing all summer, I thought we'd immortalize it. Now, you can listen forever and remember me."

With a Sharpie, I signed, *To Appoline. With affection, Bellamy, your Emily.*

Appoline held back tears as she put the CD in the stereo, pressing play.

"Dance with me," she said, holding her hand out.

"Oh, now you've decided to be sentimental?" I joked.

She rolled her eyes.

"It's been hard to be your friend when we act like lovers," I admitted lightly to her.

"Then be my lover and just act like my friend," Appoline replied.

"So, you want to hide forever?" I asked her, genuinely curious.

"Maybe when forever is over, we can be together, free as lovers and as friends," she decided.

I left it at that. Nevertheless, I took her hand and we danced while "Bridge Over Troubled Water" played seamlessly over the conversation we had with our eyes. We held our cheeks close.

I leaned my head on her shoulder. Our bodies no longer melted into one when we touched, but each acknowledged the other. There was no narration in my head this time, no imaginary friends. It was simply Appoline and I, dancing on her grandmother's veranda, hand in hand.

I wish it could have stayed like that, but alas, night came and Appoline's anxiety along with it.

"What am I going to do without you here?" she slurred when we had retreated inside.

I couldn't figure out if the wine had been extra potent, or if she had been sneaking drinks, but this was the most drunk I had ever seen her. She was normally not one to lose control.

I tried to put her to sleep, but she begged me to stay, insisting she hated being alone. She was scared, because she hated herself so much and she said she knew God hated her, too.

"But being with you almost makes the hate bearable," she told me.

Sometime after midnight, when I had gone to the kitchen to fetch some water, I realized she had slipped away again.

Collapsed on the closet floor, the wretched self-diagnosed sinner writhed in cold, heated agony. The smell of snot and vomit and unkempt thoughts and stuttered secrets revealed the mild frenzy that had erupted from the tiny box where she hid her transgressions.

I was afraid to lie down next to her this time, so I stood, taking in all that was around me. Pools of red wine sat patiently on the windowsill, longing for affection from lips that didn't mind the voracious dye of cherry flavored blood soaking through to stain the teeth hidden behind them.

Fragility masked the essence of strong liquor floating in the air. I saw the flasks littered beside Appoline on the floor. She opened her eyes when she heard me, a pathetic and pitiable sight. I was torn in despair. Was this my doing? Or was this a well-established pattern I had just happened to walk in on?

"Remember when your grandmother came and knelt beside you?" I whispered to her. "She brought you this."

I pulled the rosary from Appoline's pillow where I had left it, and I vowed to keep the anger away.

"Please, Appoline. It's going to be okay, but I need you to drink some water."

"I'm sorry," she mumbled, drinking from the pitcher I left by her side.

I continued to circle the bedroom, uncertain, yet unfortunately highly aware of the heaping mess of instability Appoline had become.

"Everyone leaves," she said, water dripping down her chin. "I'm just sad."

I nodded, understanding exactly what she meant. Holding the carpeted floor to her chest, she breathed into the ground. I saw her asking the depths of our existence to amass her drunken thoughts and coat them with beautiful lies.

This time, the morning came with objection. I had sat beside Appoline all night, praying that whatever was eating at her would subside. She was humiliated when she awoke. No matter what I said, she couldn't look me in the eye. I was sitting at the kitchen counter, wondering how things had gotten to be this way. She walked in, her hair in knots and her clothes stained with wine.

"Let's go home," she said to me.

"I-I kind of wanted to stay one more night," I told her.

"Why?" She was antsy.

"I just wanted to stay three nights, that's all." I shrugged, unable to explain how important the third night was to me.

"Well, you can stay. I need to leave."

"You're going to leave me here alone?" I asked, dumbfounded.

"I need to get away from here," she said.

"You're always needing to get away from somewhere." I rolled my eyes, annoyed with the dramatics. "Can't you just enjoy what time we have left?"

"Time we have left? You're not dying," she said.

"Fine, go. See you again in a year."

Appoline softened, her eyes warm with embarrassment.

"Here," she said, and handed me thirty francs. "Take the train back to Saint __ de Vie tomorrow when you're ready. I'll meet you at the station. I just need some time by myself. Sorry about last night."

She kissed me on the cheek and walked out the giant oak-carved front door. I would see Appoline one more time that summer, even though she stood me up and didn't arrive at the train station in Saint __ de Vie like she promised. I wrote her a letter on the train. Though there wasn't much left to be said, nor much left to be done, I wrote:

We did everything so intensely. Quickly. Passionately. Feeling everything, I had finally become submissive to the idea that loss was inevitable. Risk was inescapable, but so were your arms around my neck and I wanted them there forever. High risk, high reward.

Tracing your lips with my finger, I knew you were beautiful. I wanted you to feel it. The unruly serenity we felt in those plateaued moments of ecstasy break me now, Appoline. I lived in our joyous car rides. I lived in your honeyed-dimple kisses. I lived in the chances we gave ourselves.

We were greedy for the high we felt when my hand was on your thigh and my lips tickled your ear. We deserved it. We deserved every peak of tranquility and every stupor of silence. We deserved those moments of pure elation.

I lived in the peace your smell gave me. I lived in the drenched shirt I wore as we danced in the ocean and promised we'd never stop living. I let you splash me.

I lived with you.

It took me many years to accept that things didn't conclude poorly or blow up in our faces. In fact, they just happened to peter out, as most relationships do. I wasn't regretful of my summer in Saint __ de Vie or the friends I had made. I just wished I hadn't fallen so hard for an ending that was plausible, but not at all likely.

My mom and grandfather greeted me at the station when I arrived back at the seaside village. My mother ranted about safety and going off to foreign places without telling her first, while my grandfather chuckled lightly and handed me a croissant. When I got back to his cottage, I packed without stopping for a moment to process anything.

I didn't want to take the time to make a single additional memory. All that I had was enough. I spent the remainder of my last day in Saint __ de Vie sipping espresso with Papaly while he glanced at me with sorrow in his eyes. I scolded him for making me sad.

When the moon replaced the sun in the sky, I propped open my bedroom bay windows one last time and lay in bed, wondering why my stomach kept lurching. This was the last time things would ever be the way they were before. I was going back to New York, and I wouldn't be who I was. I didn't know when I'd be able to return. Saint __ de Vie felt like a placeholder in time, a standstill where the villagers smiled and the custard was rich, but now it was the place I left my ignorance, my innocence.

I despised Appoline for so many years to come, for forcing me to wonder if she was okay. Before her, I had known peace. After her, all I could do was think about where she was and what she was doing and if she had replaced me yet.

The night had grown quiet, when I heard shuffling in the backyard, my cue to slip out the bay windows, onto the green lawn. Just as I had guessed, Appoline lay there in the grass, looking up at the stars. I knew she would come. With my giant comforter in hand, I lay down beside her, grass tickling my cheeks. We shared the blanket.

I never gave her the letter I wrote. It was more for me, anyway. There was no need to make things hurt more than they needed to. Everything that needed to be said had already been said. Whatever was left was for the wind.

It was a clear night, and just as my summer had begun, it ended with Appoline and I lying side by side in my grandfather's backyard. The birdhouse swayed and I laughed, remembering how I thought it had been a good omen. Now, it was just a birdhouse. Maybe it was always just a birdhouse.

Appoline lay there with me for an hour or so before she squeezed my hand and got up, running away back to the hotel. Life was moving, and so was she. I boarded my plane early the next morning. I had pretzels as a snack.

When I arrived home and my dad pulled into the driveway, I saw a package out front with my name on it. Appoline had express mailed me the rosary I'd found in her closet. There was no note, but it didn't matter. I knew she had written one; she had probably just decided not to ever give it to me.

Epilogue–Ten Years Later

APPOLINE WROTE TO ME sporadically over the years, keeping me well informed of all her new adventures. I hadn't been able to visit since I left after the summer that I turned twenty-two. Appoline never made it out to New York either. Things, as they do, just happened to get busy.

The most recent postcard I received was from Ibiza, where she was enjoying a holiday with her wife, Patricia. She said their makeshift wedding was the liveliest event Saint __ de Vie had ever seen. Muriel cried when she walked down the aisle, blowing her nose so loudly, the band had to pause to let her finish. Appoline also mentioned that Papaly sat in the back, smiling proudly in his walrus hat.

"I am no longer what people perceive me to be, or what others would hope me to be. I am just Appoline. I am me," Appoline wrote in her curly penmanship. "Remember when you asked me if I ever thought I'd be happy? Well, I just wanted to let you know that I don't sleep in the closet anymore. I haven't in a very long time."

On the front of the postcard, she had scrawled in small letters, "PS I owe you many ice creams."

Papaly went back to work. He decided he couldn't sit idly by and watch Saul bounce around on his heels anxiously waiting for customers to purchase spirits that he knew nothing about. So the two partnered together, much to Saul's relief, and had a grand reopening of Aux vins de Malloren. Papaly does the talking now, and Saul just sticks to the numbers. Oh, Papaly also completed the stone-lined path in front of his cottage. Apparently, it had been finished for quite some time, it just took him a while to realize it.

François left Saint __ de Vie almost immediately after I did, needing a change of pace and women. He moved with his mother somewhere south and opened a patisserie specializing in gâteau Basque. His best flavor? Black cherry. I think he's married with children now. Maybe he's a bachelor. Either way, I'm sure he's doing just fine.

Carlo never became a captain of a ship, but he did end up traveling to Monaco, where he bought a boat and paid someone else to captain *for him. I believe he named it Carlo Junior. Unfortunately, his parents cut him off for his excessive spending. Here's hoping his crew can get him home safe without throwing him overboard.*

My mother fell back into her old ways once I started my job in New York. She moved around for a bit, uncertain where to station herself. On a self-exploration trip to Lisbon, she met a man who caught her eye. She's enamored with him, enough to keep a home and career in Portugal. She also writes me letters. Her passion, she's found, is helping lone tourists make their way through the city. It doesn't pay much, but it satiates her need to stay busy. She still wears a bikini at sixty with no shame; the tourists love this.

New York City can be a lonely place for someone who spends too much time in her own head. That's why I live in Bar Harbor now. After my brief job as a magazine editor, I began working in a flower shop while writing my novel about my time spent in France.

In the matter of my romantic life, I've learned that people never cease to disappoint. I've had two serious relationships and a few two-night stands. I never was a one-night stand type of girl. I'm on my own right now, but that's okay. I have my flowers. There's no rush. After allowing myself to cry, I pinned Appoline's postcard on my closet door where her rosary beads still hang, a beautiful reminder that, like her, I am me.

As for Louie, I heard he's still holding down La Baleine Bleue. His hair has gone fully grey, and he has a touch of arthritis in his pouring hand now, but he's not one to complain. He can be found behind the bar every evening, serving drinks to the rowdy and handsome people of Saint __ de Vie, as the burgundy sky paints itself black and the waves croon the villagers to sleep.

About Emily Fohr

After graduating from Arizona State University in 2018 with a degree in broadcast journalism, Emily moved out to Los Angeles on a whim. Currently, she works as an assistant to a producer in the film industry, and her original screenplay, PURLIEU, placed as a semi-finalist in the 2019 San Francisco International Screenwriting Competition. This past year, she completed her first novel, an LGBTQ+ story written with honesty and expression, much of it deriving from true experiences of her time spent on the Côte de Lumière.

Connect with Emily

Email: emilyfohr@gmail.com

Instagram: @elimufohr

Twitter: @emily_fohr

Note to Readers:

Thank you for reading a book from Desert Palm Press. We appreciate you as a reader and want to ensure you enjoy the reading process. We would like you to consider posting a review on your preferred media sites and/or your blog or website.

For more information on upcoming releases, author interviews, contests, giveaways and more, please sign up for our newsletter and visit us at Desert Palm Press: www.desertpalmpress.com and "Like" us on Facebook: Desert Palm Press.

Bright Blessings

Made in USA - Kendallville, IN
88107_9781948327596
05.18.2022 1156